Book News

Sign up for exclusive updates and offers at
news.jljarvis.com

Get the Audiobook

The Return

The Return

Highland Soldiers 3

J.L. Jarvis

BOOKBINDER PRESS

THE RETURN
Highland Soldiers 3

ISBN (ebook) 978-0-9906476-2-1
ISBN (paperback) 978-0-9906476-3-8
ISBN (audiobook) 978-1-942767-30-5

Published by BookbinderPress.com

Chapter 1

The Soldier's Return

AUTUMN 1680

"Poor man, look at you!" Mari called from the foot of the stairs. Her deep-brown hair was pulled back into a knot at the base of her neck, and her gray dress was fitted and plain. The morning light from the window above caught her moss-green eyes and her warm, gentle smile. "You must have been tired."

Alex's gaze softened as he combed his fingers through his wild, sand-colored hair. "Aye, hen, I was. Thank you for letting me sleep here. I'll not have so nice a bed waiting at home."

"Oh, but you will. I've sent two maids over to make your house ready." She turned and began dusting a table.

"*Och*, you're too good to me, Mari. Callum doesnae deserve you. I, on the other hand, do." He winked. "And you! You deserve a *braw*, charming laddie like me." He arrived at the bottom step and leaned his brawny frame over the rail as though he might kiss her.

Mari swatted him with her dust cloth. "And you deserve something, but I'll not tell you what."

"I will." Callum strode in, tall and robust, with his dark hair tied back. He went straight to Mari, took the dust cloth from her hand, and set it on the hall table, out of her reach, with a warm but admonishing smile.

Mari smiled in return, a tinge of guilt in her eyes.

Callum's eyes flickered toward Alex. "What's he done now?"

"He's being himself."

Not surprised and just slightly amused, Callum looked at Alex then turned his dark eyes to his wife. "I've been trying to cure him of that since we were lads."

"I've nae doubt, but there's no hope for that one." Mari shook her head and smiled as she walked down the hall toward the kitchen. "You're both hungry, I'm guessing?" When they entered the kitchen, Mari began cooking the eggs she had brought in earlier from the byre.

"And just where are the servants I employ to do the cooking and cleaning?" asked Callum.

Mari shrugged. "I sent them on a wee errand. They'll be back soon."

"An errand? What errand?"

Mari tilted her head and exhaled. "If you must know, I sent them to Alex's house."

Callum folded his arms and glared at his friend. "Alex's house."

Alex shrugged innocently, and Mari rushed to his defense. "Dinnae blame him. It was my idea."

Alex smiled warmly at Mari and winked.

Callum sat at the long wooden table and breathed in the aroma of Mari's cooking. "Alex, now that you're home, perhaps it's time you stop flirting with my wife and find one of your own."

"Flirting?" Alex feigned innocence, but with a gleam in his eye. "Mari, was I flirting with you?"

Mari went on cooking and answered over her shoulder, "No, Alex. You were simply doing your best to vex Callum."

Alex laughed. "*Och*, Mari, now you've just made it worse."

Callum leaned back with a smug grin. "I cannae be vexed when I feel so sorry for you."

"Oh? Well, I thank you for that." Alex narrowed his eyes.

Mari spoke in an overly casual tone while she worked at the stove. "Alex, you remember Kenna, do you not?"

When Alex didn't answer right away, Callum said, "Her land borders yours."

Alex shrugged and leaned his sturdy arms on the table. "Aye, the wee lass who used to go along with the boys when we hunted and fished."

Callum folded his arms and leaned back, stretching out his long legs and crossing them at the ankle. "She hunted and fished as well as any of us—and as I recall, better than you." He raised an eyebrow at Alex.

Annoyed, Alex scowled. "Once or twice, perhaps—when I was ill. But neither woman nor man can match me, and you ken it."

Callum let out a disparaging laugh. "I ken naught

of the kind. But I will tell you this: that wee lass you speak of has grown up a bit."

Mari's faint smile faded. "Her brother's been ailing since he came home from the fighting."

Alex balked. "He had a wee scratch."

Mari said, "His wee scratch has festered, and it willnae heal. Kenna's tending to him and doesnae want to leave him alone. Would you mind stopping by to see if she needs anything?"

Alex stole a glance to be sure Callum was watching then offered his most charming look, his green eyes dancing. "For you, Mari, aye."

Callum grunted a good-natured warning to Alex while Mari set down a plate full of bannocks and smiled at her husband. Alex grabbed one and took a bite.

Mari said, "Do you think I'll have time to get you your own plate before you're through eating?"

Alex stopped, mouth full, and swallowed. "Sorry, hen. I'm a loathsome beast."

"You are," she agreed but with a hint of a smile. "But you're our loathsome beast, and we love you."

Minutes later, Alex was eagerly eating his first homemade meal in weeks. Mari and Callum became absorbed in a discussion about an upcoming party while Alex's mind wandered, and with it went his false cheer.

Mari noticed and kept glancing over, increasingly troubled, until Callum put his hand over hers and gave his head a slight shake to signal her not to pursue it. As Mari rose, her chair scraped over the wood floor and forced Alex back from his thoughts.

He said, "I must be on my way now." He stood and shook Callum's hand and gave Mari a hug as he thanked her and left.

As MUCH AS Alex treasured his friends, trying to be the same Alex they knew took wearying effort. He was no longer that man. Sometimes he thought that his heart had grown cold from the things he had seen, but the nightmares always came back and forced him to feel the same jarring emotions. Soldiers always saw things in battle, but this had been worse, for their fight had gone into homes.

Once more, the Covenanter family flashed through his mind as he'd seen them that day and would forever remember them. Oh, the man had been guilty, and yes, the Highland Host possessed legal authority to do what they had done and continued to do. Extrajudicial executions saved time and sent a strong message. But it was Alex who had fired the shot, and it was his ears that echoed with the wife's wretched sob. The faces of the children as they watched the blood drain from their father would haunt him the most. Alex had followed his orders and served his king well. Alex MacDonell was a soldier, and a good one.

Too late, he realized that he should have come home from the lowlands with Callum and Mari. After Duncan and his wife had gone to Ireland and made a home there, Callum and Mari, along with most of the Highlanders, had gone home. But Alex and Charlie stayed on for no better reason than the pay and the women. It now seemed like such a long time since he and Charlie had caroused with no cares. Once they were assigned to John Graham of Claverhouse, 1st Viscount Dundee, everything changed. Before long, Dundee would be better known as Bloody Clavers.

But that was in the past, where Alex needed to keep it. He was home in the Highlands, where he would rebuild his life.

His home wasn't far from Callum and Mari's, but he had arrived late at night. Bone tired, he had stopped for a drink and accepted the offer to sleep in Callum's fine home before completing his journey. In truth, Alex had not been in a hurry to go home, for it was full of memories he wasn't ready to face. The family he had loved there was gone.

Alex passed Mari's maids, who were on their way home on foot, and he thanked them for cleaning his house. Judging by their flirtatious grins, they were more than happy to help in that and other ways—an idea to which Alex was not necessarily averse. But that would have to wait for another day, for he longed to finish his journey. He stopped at a crossroads and sat astride his horse, gazing at his home. It wouldn't be the same. Smallpox had swept through and taken his parents and sister before he'd gone away. Barely a home had been left untouched. He had one brother left, who now lived at the castle. Callum's father, the chief, had taken him in and would train him, as he had Alex.

He took in the sight of his empty home. Shaded by large oaks, it looked over the loch. Alex took in a deep breath, then he headed the opposite way toward the humble McCowan farm. He arrived at the open doorway and stopped. The fire had dwindled to embers, leaving the smell of burnt peat rising in ribbons of smoke to waft over the unnatural stillness. On the bed lay Roddy McCowan, and on the floor beside him sat Kenna, holding her brother's hand to her tear-stained cheek. Russet hair fell in thick waves over shoulders clad in a white linen nightdress.

Reluctant to disturb her, but also not wanting to startle her, Alex quietly said, "Kenna."

She flinched and turned. But beyond the initial recognition of her name, her pale-gray eyes seemed hollow and lost. She turned back to her brother. Soft wisps of hair brushed her face, and Alex felt an impulse to brush them away just to see if her skin felt as soft as it looked. But in the midst of the thought, he sensed something was wrong. He stepped closer until he could see Roddy's face. He had watched too many men die in battle not to recognize the look of a man whose spirit had gone.

Alex lifted a quilt from another bed and tenderly wrapped it over Kenna's shoulders. She stiffened for a fleeting moment then clutched the folds of the quilt to her face and trembled as she silently wept. Alex crouched beside her, but she turned from him to blot her face and try to regain control of herself.

He gave her shoulder a tender squeeze. "It's all right to cry."

Kenna lifted her shining eyes to meet his, and the aching sorrow there struck him like a blow to the chest. Without thought, he swept her into his arms, or perhaps she flew to him. The movement was too fast and instinctive to say. He just knew that he wanted to take all her grief and carry its weight. She was too gentle to bear such a burden.

She felt so cold. Alex unclasped the brooch on his shoulder and loosened his plaid to wrap it around Kenna. She relaxed against him as she leaned her forehead against his chest and sobbed.

Alex was content just to hold her and help her to let out her grief. Shifting the weight from his knees, he sat on the floor with her on his lap. He held her as one might hold a child, which was how he had always regarded her. She had been like a sister to all of them over the years, but the soft curves of her body pressed against his made him all too aware that she had grown to a woman. His body responded to hers.

Grief had torn down the walls of propriety, leaving Kenna's emotions exposed. In that state, she clung to Alex. Seeking closeness was a natural instinct when the death of a loved one was so new and raw. Grief opened the soul and left it unprotected and desperate for comfort. In the absence of true intimacy, passion was often enough to assuage the first throes of grief as if, by clinging to life, one could block out the still vivid face of death. Alex knew that firsthand. He'd seen many men fresh from battle find solace in the arms of a willing woman.

But that knowledge should have put Alex on his guard. When Kenna put her arms around his neck and her cheek brushed his lips, he stopped thinking. His lips sought hers in a way they had no right to do. And he kissed her. The first time could have been excused as accidental—perhaps even chaste. But her lips parted, and their next kiss was anything but innocent.

Their actions were understandable for Kenna, but unforgivably selfish of Alex. She was in shock and bereft and would naturally cling to what comfort she found, but Alex had no excuse. It was one thing for a soldier to go to a brothel after battle, whether for the release of unspeakable strain, for comfort, or to simply escape. But to seize a friend's vulnerable moment of grief was contemptible.

He pulled away and held her face while he shook his head. "I'm sorry."

"I'm not!"

She tried to kiss him again, but he gripped her shoulders and pushed her away. Her soft gray eyes pleaded for comfort that he dared not give. She tugged at his soul. He had always enjoyed women—at times too much for his own good—but he had never been a vile rogue. Kenna stirred his desire, but she stirred his heart too, which was a new sensation for him. So as she searched his eyes with unabashed longing, Alex kissed her again, and he let his hands claim her body. Each touch made him ache to get closer. His nerves pulsed with desire that, moments ago, he had been determined to resist.

Alex stood abruptly, breathing deeply and shaking his head. "This is not what you need."

"How do you ken what I need?"

Her wounded expression struck a sharper blow than any he'd felt from a dirk, but he turned from her nevertheless. As he walked through the doorway, her words rang in his ears.

"Alex, don't leave me alone."

SEVERAL DAYS LATER, the men buried Roddy in the hillside graveyard alongside Kenna's mother and father. She was now the only one of their family left behind with the living. As was the custom, the women did not attend the burial but stayed behind and prepared for the feast that would follow. Kenna cooked into the late afternoon until one of the older women from the village sent her outside for some air. When she stepped through the doorway, she saw Alex sitting on a bench near the door.

When he saw her, he stood. "They're burying him now. I was worried about you, so I came back ahead of the others."

Kenna started to say something, but Mari called for Kenna and appeared on the threshold in search of her.

"I'm sorry. Am I interrupting?" Mari looked from one to the other. The tension between them was palpable. "Aye, I can see that I am." She disappeared inside the cottage.

Kenna returned his gaze with a blank expression then followed Mari inside.

"I'm sorry," said Mari.

Kenna said, "Dinnae be. It was nothing."

Mari eyed her skeptically. "Are you all right?"

"Aye," she answered without thinking. "Well, no. 'Tis a hard thing to lose a brother. We grew up together. We played, and we fought. When everyone else was gone and we had only each other, we promised we would never leave one another alone. But

promises get broken, and people are left to go on."
Kenna had already run out of tears.

Mari glanced about the small cottage and clasped
Kenna's hand. "Why don't you come stay with us for a
while?"

"That's kind of you, but I'll be fine." Kenna smiled
warmly.

Mari nodded. "I understand. Just know that if you
change your mind, we're not far away."

"Thank you." Kenna's eyes shone with her last
remnants of tears.

In the gloaming, guests shifted from eating to
drinking, and Kenna drifted away for a moment alone.
Away from the house and beyond the byre was an oak
large enough to hide behind, which she often had done
as a child. Too late, she discovered that someone else
had had the same idea.

"Alex."

"Aye."

After the moment it took her to recover, she said,
"I'm sorry," and spun to walk back to the house.

"Don't go." He grasped her upper arm.

Her breath caught for a moment, but she managed
to say, "I recall saying the same to you once, but you
left anyway—as will I." She pulled away, but he held
fast.

"Kenna, wait. I'm sorry."

In the midst of the grief she was drowning in, his
words held little power. For a long while, all she
could do was stare at him. "What is it you want?
Whatever it is, I have nothing left, so please leave me
alone."

In an instant, he released her. "The last thing I want is to hurt you."

"And yet it's the first thing you do every time." Kenna went back to the cottage.

THE NEXT AFTERNOON, Kenna stood in Callum and Mari's front hallway with a bundle in her hand. Mari hastened to welcome her.

Kenna said, "May I take you up on your offer to visit for a few days?"

"Of course! I'm so glad you're here!" She took Kenna's bundle of clothing and handed it to a housemaid with instructions to take it to a guest room. Then Mari hooked her arm in Kenna's and led her to the drawing room.

Kenna saw Callum first as he sat facing the fire, then two men stood and turned toward them. Alex's eyes darted from Mari to Kenna, where they remained focused upon her.

Mari turned to Kenna. "Callum and Alex have just come back from fishing, so we'll have a fine feast for supper."

Kenna's cheeks, still flushed from her vigorous ride in the crisp autumn air, reddened more as Alex greeted her with a marked reserve. Mari shot her husband a glance but got an unhelpful shrug. Doing her best to hide her dismay, Kenna forced a small nod for the two men. A chill wind from the north couldn't have done a better job at bringing conversation to a halt.

Mari broke the uncomfortable silence. "Callum,

I'm having second thoughts about what to serve with the salmon."

He frowned as if she had gone mad.

"I need your advice. Come with me, and I'll show you."

He opened his mouth, but the pointed look she shot at him stopped him. He rose to go with her, offering a quiet, "Excuse me."

He needn't have bothered—neither guest seemed aware he had said it. Kenna appeared frozen where Mari had left her.

"Please sit down." Alex offered his seat.

Kenna absently thanked him and sat. Drawn to the warmth of the fire and away from Alex, she stared at the flames.

He glanced toward the door, which Mari had discreetly closed. "Kenna, I'm sorry. When I first saw you, we were both in shock and not thinking. Forgive me."

"Of course." Her voice sounded sweet, but her manner was icy.

Alex rubbed the back of his neck. "You've been on my mind."

For the first time since she walked in, Kenna let her eyes drift to his. She may as well have looked into the sun for the burning pain he brought her.

Alex leaned in closer. "I've thought about you— worried—these past days, but I thought calling on you would only make it worse."

With a nod, Kenna looked away. Her emotions were caught in her throat, and she knew speaking would only advertise those feelings she wanted to hide.

Alex laid his hand on the arm of her chair—so close she felt the heat of his body but not close enough for his warmth to surround her. She longed to lean into it.

He said, "I hope we can be friends like we once were."

"Were we ever friends?" It came out almost a whisper.

"Well, not like Callum and the other lads, but I'd like to think that we were—and still are. Please look upon me as your friend."

"I will try."

The fact that he had said it so kindly made her ache even more, for Alex had no idea how much she had always loved him. Long before Roddy's death, he had broken her heart, and his kissing her had merely opened the wound. His every effort toward kindness only hurt more. He would keep hurting her without ever realizing it.

ALEX AND CALLUM went fishing again in the morning, leaving Kenna and Mari alone for breakfast.

Mari took a sip then set down her teacup. "I might be overstepping, but has Alex wronged you somehow? I couldn't help but notice a tension between you last night."

Kenna wanted to deny it, but she couldn't lie to Mari. Since Mari's arrival at Invergarry, they had become friends, and she knew she could trust Mari to keep a confidence. "He's done nothing wrong."

"But there's something between you."

"No, not really." As she said it, she recalled the feel of his lips when he kissed her. "I'm afraid it was all my doing. One day I was a girl following the boys so I could do the fun things they did, and the next I became a young woman. But no one noticed, least of all Alex, because by then I was one of the lads. I'm not even sure when it happened, but at some point, I let myself love him. I knew that he felt nothing for me, but I hoped with the fervor of a person too young to know that hope comes in finite amounts. Does anyone understand that before it's too late? I suppose I broke my own heart—a wiser girl would have guarded herself from such feelings."

Mari fixed her soft gaze on her friend. "And you love him still?"

Kenna shook her head. "I didnae think that I did. While he was gone, I convinced myself that those feelings were over."

"And then he came back." Mari sighed in sympathy. "Feelings can change."

Kenna said, "Not his."

Mari stared at her teacup. "I got to know Alex when he and the lads served under Callum. But of course you know that. I believe I know Alex quite well. He's full of mischief sometimes—or rather, he used to be. Since he's come home, he's been different. But he has a good heart."

Kenna nodded. "Aye, he does, and I ken it would sorely grieve him to think that he'd hurt me."

Mari continued, "And that heart has a soft spot for you. I see it when he looks at you."

"Aye. But you see, there are all kinds of love; my heart wants the one that it cannae have."

"For now, perhaps."

Kenna shook her head. "The night before they all left for the lowlands, everyone gathered to wish them well." Kenna's eyes shone as she recalled it. "What a fine evening it was! All moon and stars in a dark blanket of sky, and the fire glowed as the men danced the sword dance. Then everyone danced, and music filled the air and our hearts, and it felt like the souls of our people were joined. I'd never wanted to dance before then, so I'd never learned how. But then, all I wanted was to be close to him. A dance would have given me that chance.

"All evening, he laughed and had fun, but he had paid me no heed. I wanted so for him to look at me and really see me." A slight smile crossed her face. "So I gathered the courage to walk up to him—just to talk and be with him. By then, he'd had a wee bit to drink, so it wasnae hard to get him talking. Then a pretty girl came along and asked him to dance. He excused himself—very kindly, for that's how he is—and they were gone." Kenna stared into the fire. Her emotions rose to the surface, but she tamped them down. "The last time I saw him that evening, she was hanging on his arm, and they went for a walk to the woods. The rest you can guess for yourself, as I have."

"I'm so sorry." Mari touched Kenna's hand sympathetically.

With a dismissive wave, Kenna said, "'Tis foolish. He did nothing to wrong me. But I loved him, and my heart broke just the same. But I grew stronger from it, and I swore—" Kenna glanced downward. "I ken that it's wicked to swear, but I did. I swore that I would never let anyone close to my heart, for it gives them the power to hurt."

Mari shook her head. "The right man can fill your heart and protect it. Dinnae cheat yourself out of that!"

"The more you love someone, the more they can hurt you. I loved him too much." She spoke softly, as though it pained her even to voice those words.

"Oh, Kenna, give someone time to know you and love you."

"No man will ever love me like that." Kenna took a deep breath and exhaled. "Well, there it is. I've held it inside for so long. I have friends, but no one I felt I could talk to like this. I'm glad that you know, and I'm glad for your friendship."

"And I, yours." Mari put her hand over Kenna's and gave it a squeeze. While Kenna dried her eyes, Mari glanced at the window. "Look at the leaves. We should go for a walk and enjoy all the colors. We'll have precious few days like this before winter sets in."

After washing their teacups, they donned their arisaids and went outside together.

THE TWO MEN led their horses to the burn for water, then waded in and cast their fishing lines.

Callum said, "Are you going to tell me what happened last night?" His eyes revealed a tinge of amusement.

Alex shrugged. "I dinnae ken what you mean." Alex wasn't one to lie. The truth was he couldn't forget kissing Kenna or the guilt he felt after, but there was nothing to be gained by sharing that with Callum.

Callum grinned. "Oh? Well, from my point of view, you went daft at the sight of that lass."

"At whom—wee Kenna?"

"Wee Kenna isnae so wee anymore."

Alex gave a nonchalant nod.

"She's a grown woman."

"Aye." Alex fixed his eyes straight ahead.

Silence had almost settled between them when Callum said, "She's a bonny lass, aye?"

Gritting his teeth, Alex grunted in agreement.

"That deep-red hair—long and thick. You could take it in handfuls and lose yourself in it," said Callum with a glint in his eye.

Alex knew Callum too well to fall into his trap. With as serious an expression as he could muster, Alex said, "Aye, but do you not think Mari would mind?"

Callum hit Alex's arm with the back of his hand. "For you—not for me! *Och*! I'm just trying to help you."

"Dinnae trouble yourself."

"All right, but 'tis a painful sight to behold."

"Is it? 'Tis a shame you're in pain, for I'm not." Alex glanced at him sideways, then returned his attention to fishing. But his thoughts were with Kenna.

Chapter 2

The Lesson

AND STEP, TOGETHER, STEP—AND STEP, TOGETHER, step...

After they finished the dance and sat to rest, Mari listed the dances she and Kenna had practiced so far. "Mind, I'm no expert. I've only been learning to dance them since I married Callum and moved here from the lowlands."

"Did they not have dancing there?"

Mari's eyes opened wide as she shook her head. "Not in my home."

Only then did Kenna remember that Mari had been a Covenanter whose kirk frowned upon dancing. When she fell in love with Callum, an enemy soldier, she had turned from her religion, knowing her family would have no more to do with her.

"But you're from here," Mari said. "How is it you never learned to dance?"

Kenna shrugged. "I never wanted to. I suppose it's because I grew up in a house with two men. My mother died giving birth to me. My brother was older, so he taught me to fish, hunt, and ride. *Och*, my brother and I used to have such fun!" Her eyes lost their spark as she thought of Roddy.

Mari looked puzzled. "But all the lads here seem to ken how to dance."

With a faint smile, Kenna said, "Aye. The first time I tried to dance—we were just children, ken? But he laughed."

"Who laughed?"

Kenna wished she hadn't said anything about it, but she had, so she answered. "Alex." She waved to dismiss it.

"Alex? He's not one to be cruel."

"Oh, no! I'm sure he didn't mean to be, but I was such a terrible dancer. How could he not laugh? Anyway, after that, if anyone asked, I just said that I didnae like dancing. In time, they stopped asking." Kenna averted her eyes from Mari's sympathetic gaze.

"I'm sure Alex would feel terrible now if he knew how he'd hurt you." Mari's eyes twinkled. "If he doesn't, I'm sure I could bring that about."

After they had a good laugh, Kenna said, "It was so long ago. He's a fine man now."

"Aye." Mari's smile faded. "I do worry about him all alone in that house."

Kenna stared at the window. "I dinnae think Alex minds being alone."

Mari nodded. "Now if it were Charlie, the poor man would go mad." Mari laughed as she shook her head.

Kenna agreed. "There's nothing that man enjoys

more than being surrounded by people—preferably women."

"I don't suppose there was a young lady involved in his decision to stay behind in the lowlands." Kenna smiled.

Mari said, "You do know Charlie."

Kenna rolled her eyes and laughed. "Aye, but anyone could gather as much within minutes of meeting the man."

"True enough."

The two women grew wistful as they thought of their friends who had gone off to the lowlands. Mari had gotten to know them after she'd met Callum, but he and Alex were the only ones who came home. Duncan and his wife had fled to Ireland following a conflict with his superior officer, young Hugh died while away, and Hugh's brother, Charlie, volunteered to stay on after most of the men had gone home.

Mari clapped her hands on her knees and stood. "So what other dances shall we practice?"

They struggled through three of the more difficult dances before Kenna collapsed in a chair. "Mari, you have the patience of Job, but I'm hopeless!"

"No, you're not. Let's try again." She reached out to pull Kenna from the chair, but Mari's eyes brightened when Callum peeked inside and, seeing them dancing, disappeared. Before Kenna could stop her, she called to Callum, "Come help with this dance!" Mari reached the doorway and stopped short. "Oh, I didn't realize Alex was with you."

With a straight face, Callum said, "*Och*, what a pity! I was just on my way out." Only Alex saw

Callum's mouth curve up on the side. "But I can spare Alex. He's a much better dancer than I!"

Without waiting for a response, Callum escaped through a doorway with only a snort to betray his suppressed laughter. Mari stood in the doorway, smiling sweetly at Alex, while a mortified Kenna waited inside. Alex shut his eyes and cursed Callum under his breath then proceeded down the hall. Mari turned just long enough to offer Kenna an apologetic shrug.

As Alex entered the room, Mari said, "We're planning a céilidh at the end of the month. I know that Kenna won't quite be out of mourning by then but only by a few days. I think it would do her good to join us. But she's never danced."

"Never?" asked Alex.

Kenna inwardly groaned but forced herself to meet his eyes. "I never bothered to learn."

Alex looked at her with those green eyes that softened the heart she was trying to harden. "I'll teach you."

Kenna frowned. "Really, it's not necessary."

"I know, but I want to." He held out his hand, and she took it.

Alex sang as they practiced the steps. Every time Kenna missed a step, she wanted to stop.

Alex said, "We all make mistakes, but you've got to keep going. Come, let's try it again."

He offered his palms, and she put her hands on them. He walked her through the combinations, guiding her and quietly coaching each step and change in direction. As she concentrated on his instruction,

Kenna found herself moving in sync with him. She nearly forgot about guarding her heart and allowed the steps and rhythm to sweep her away. For the first time in her life, she felt as though she might learn to dance, and she felt almost at ease with Alex.

At some point, Mari stepped out of the room. Sometime later, the awkwardness between them faded. They were dancing and managed to laugh now and then.

At the end of the dance, Alex said, "Now you curtsy, and I'll bow."

Kenna almost felt normal until, as directed, she rose from her curtsy. He lifted his eyes as he rose from his bow, and they met face-to-face. Neither moved.

"That was fine." Alex straightened with a gentle smile. His eyes held hers once again.

Kenna decided it must be the light that made his eyes shine soft and green, his mane of disheveled, straw-colored hair roughly framing his face. She wanted to run her fingers through it to put it in order.

"See? You're learning." He narrowed his eyes with a confident nod.

"Aye, well, we'll see." Kenna averted her eyes like a shy schoolgirl and felt foolish for doing so. She felt color tint her cheeks. She had always blushed easily, but never did she regret it as much as she did then.

She lifted her eyes to glance at him, but she was drawn in again by his steady gaze. He appeared somehow lost, and she wanted to help him find his way. As if sensing her thoughts, perhaps even her feelings, Alex lowered his eyes. Kenna followed his gaze to her hand. He had taken it as she rose from the curtsy, and he still held it. His thumb slid over her skin. That, and the way that he studied her, made her heart pound. His hand slipped from hers.

"I should be on my way home." His eyes darted toward the door, and the spell broke.

Her voice came out softly. "I'm sorry you had to do this."

Alex said, "I'm not, and I could have said no."

He gave her a gentle smile laced with regret and lingered as though he might say something else. If he meant to, he changed his mind, for he muttered good-bye and left. Kenna touched the place on her hand he had touched and gazed at the doorway.

When she was sure he was gone, she went up to her bedroom and sat on the bed with a sigh. "No." She sank back onto the bed and looked at the canopy. "I willnae love him again." She shut her eyes, her words just a whisper. "I cannae love him still."

Chapter 3

The Encumbrance

KENNA STOOD ON A CHAIR THE NEXT MORNING AND tried not to fidget while Mari measured and pinned up her hem. Kenna wore a forest-green jacket, a neckerchief of white linen, a beige vest, a petticoat with matching green stripes, and a white linen apron.

"'Tis bonny, Kenna. You've done a fine job."

"Aye, well, my mother had this material in a trunk. She was planning to make a new dress before she died, and I never had the heart to cut into the cloth. But I think she would like that I've finished what she started."

"She would have loved seeing how pretty it looks on you. The green sets off your red hair."

Kenna smiled. "It's been a long time since I've had a new dress. I have to admit that I like it."

"So will the lads," Mari said with a nod.

"I only care about one." Kenna sighed. "But I'll soon have to be practical. I cannae run a farm all alone."

"While it's good to be practical, as your friend, I wish you love."

"You've been lucky, Mari. You've found what many women dream of."

Mari leveled somber eyes on Kenna. "It was not without cost. But I can tell you this: no matter how hard it might be, love is worth it." Mari smoothed out the hem, took one last look, and gave an approving nod. "Well, we'd best get to work. You've a dress to hem, and I've a céilidh to plan!"

THREE WEEKS PASSED, during which time Kenna managed to avoid Alex, except for brief greetings and cordial words when he happened to pass by her cottage. She tried to convince herself that it was better that way, but that only drove her emotions into a barely controllable fervor when she caught fleeting glimpses of him.

But a day came when she was summoned to the great hall of the castle to stand before the Glengarry, Chief of the MacDonells of Glengarry and Callum's father. Callum and Mari stood in the back of the hall, when Alex slipped in and joined them. When her name was called, Kenna steeled herself and stepped forward.

Glengarry sat in an impressive chair on the dais, but he was most impressive. Despite his age, he had an imposing presence, with broad shoulders, bold features, and brown hair salted with gray. He regarded her kindly. "Mistress McCowan, I'm sorry about your brother. He was a fine lad who fought well for the clan."

"Thank you, sir."

He frowned as he studied her. "There's a matter concerning the land. At the suggestion of my son, Callum, I'd intended to grant you a life estate in the land that has always been your home."

"Thank you, sir." She exhaled in relief.

Glengarry held up his palm. "Hear me out, lass."

She hastened to say, "I'm sorry." She gripped a small bit of her apron without realizing it at first.

Glengarry went on. "While small farms are usually owned by the Laird and leased to tenants by a tacksman, yours is a somewhat unusual case. 'Tis quite a long tale. To be honest, we've had a devil of a time sorting it out, but the essence is this: Generations ago, one of my ancestors honored a clansman with a parcel of land. That land fell into the hands of another family through marriage. The owner, for reasons no one remembers, granted a small parcel of that land to a farmer—your grandfather—but to keep it in the family, the land was encumbered with a fee tail male."

Kenna wanted to tell him to stop. She understood only enough to be sure his news would be bad. Her ears rang, and her head swam.

"Your father never owned the land outright. His fee tail could only pass from one male heir to the next. Your brother was the last male heir in your family."

The mention of her brother brought her sorrow back to the surface and clouded her thinking.

Glengarry chose his words carefully and spoke

gently. "With your brother being the last male heir, the land now reverts to the grantor."

"The grantor?" Kenna listened with growing apprehension.

Glengarry said, "Please know that you've a home in this castle as long as you live. You need never fear that. As for the original grantor, we've found an old deed. The land was granted to your great-grandfather by the owner of a neighboring property." Glengarry searched the room and called, "Alex MacDonell, would you step forward, please?"

Kenna turned to see a stunned Alex. He came forward and stood beside her.

Glengarry said, "Alex MacDonell, you're the heir of the original grantor. With the passing of the last male heir to the McCowan farm, the land reverts back to you as the surviving descendant of the original grantor. In short, you now own the McCowan farm. My solicitor has drawn up a document to formalize the reversion of the title to you. Come forward and sign it."

Kenna wanted to run outside and ride away as far as she could go, but instead, she watched Alex take ownership of her home. He had already broken her heart—now he had taken her home. She had nothing left.

When he had finished signing, Alex turned and walked toward her. "Lass?"

Kenna looked past him to Glengarry. "Thank you, sir." She walked out of the great hall, leaving Alex behind.

Heat burned her cheeks as she got onto Roddy's horse and rode away across land she had known all of her life. She arrived at the simple cottage that had been her home—until today. Once inside, she collapsed on the box bed and wept. Minutes later, she heard a horse, then footsteps approaching. Alex knocked on the door and said her name so gently, it angered her. How could he still affect her? After all that had happened, her heart still sprang to life at the sound of his voice, and it made the stabbing pain even worse.

"Kenna."

She stared at the door. It was his door now, and his home. She rose from the bed and opened the door. "I can't even ask you to leave, for you've more right to be here than I." He stepped toward her, but she met him with a cold stare. "No. Please go. I'll pack my belongings and be gone in the morning."

"No." He put his hands on her shoulders, but she turned her cheek toward him. "Kenna."

She struggled against his firm grip. "Just leave me alone!"

"I can't! Let me help you." He struggled to hold her, but she thrashed and pounded his chest.

"I don't want your help! Why won't you just leave me alone?"

He managed to circle his arms about her, but holding her against him took a vise grip. "Because I care about you."

She was no match for his powerful arms, so she buried her head in his chest and cried, "Do you? Well, I despise you!" She pounded a fist against his chest.

"You've taken it all—everything that has mattered to me."

He said her name in deep, soothing tones as his cheek brushed against her soft hair. Kenna clung to her anger, but it slipped away with each tender touch. She was open and raw as a wound. There wasn't anything anyone could do that wouldn't hurt her to the core, so she leaned against him, too weary to fight anymore.

When she spoke, she barely recognized her own voice. It was cold and detached. "And now you've taken my dignity too."

She lifted her face and took in the ordinary things in her home. Three chairs, now empty, faced the fireplace. She could almost see the people who'd once sat in each one. An impossible longing for how things once were overwhelmed her until she had to turn to the door. As she did, her eyes met his.

In words both deliberate and quiet, she said, "You may own everything I have, but you do not own me. Please take your hands off me, and don't touch me again." She held his gaze and felt pleased for the pain she saw that she had inflicted.

Alex did as she asked then closed the door gently behind him.

THE NEXT MORNING, he went to check on her, but Kenna was gone. Alex rode over to Callum's for help. While Callum saddled his horse, Alex said, "She was angry and sent me away. I thought she might listen to me in the morning, so I left her to calm down. But this morning, the cottage was empty, and her horse was gone."

Callum finished cinching his horse. "I dinnae think she would go far."

"And why wouldn't she?" Alex's narrowed his eyes as he forced back his anger. "I drove her away. She told me to leave, but I wouldnae listen to her."

"Calm yourself, man. Kenna's too smart to do anything as daft as running away. She's likely gone somewhere to think."

That made sense. Alex focused his thoughts. "I hope you're right. But where would she go?"

"Where did she used to go when she wanted to be alone?" His face lit up. "The bank of the loch?"

Alex shook his head. "She knows we would look for her there."

"Even if she's not running away, she rode, so it's no use looking too close to home."

Alex nodded. "She'd not go toward the village. There's too much blether about her. She'd want to avoid it."

"So we'll head for the opposite direction."

"Aye," Alex said, as he mounted his horse.

Mari joined them with two bundles and a bottle of whisky. "There are bannocks here. I thought you might split up, so I've wrapped them separately."

Callum thanked her and gave her a hug.

Meanwhile, Alex thought of all the places they used to go when they were younger. "I think I ken where she might be. I'm going up to the ridge."

"I'll try the rest," Callum said.

Alex said, "I'll be back before dark."

"If we haven't found her by dark, I'll gather some men to set out in the morning to search."

They headed away in opposite directions. Alex thought of a time they had visited the cleft in the ridge overlooking their homes. She was thirteen, and he had thought himself a fully grown man at seventeen.

YOUNG ALEX and Kenna looked down at their farms. Kenna leaned her back against the trunk of a tree. "You cannae tell where one begins and the other ends."

Alex said, "Yes, you can. That tree there marks one edge. If you draw a line from the jutting rock over there, that's the line."

"*Och*, Alex! You're always so sure of yourself." Kenna moved a few inches away and leaned back against the tree, her arms folded.

"I am when I'm right—which is all of the time." Alex laughed and jumped up to grab a tree limb. He swung back and forth a few times then dropped to the ground.

"We could settle it all if the two farms got married. Then the two would become one." Kenna laughed.

"You're an *eejit*."

Kenna shrugged, pushed off the tree with her foot, and walked away.

She had taken him to that clearing. She had found it herself, and she wanted to show it to him. Alex wished he could go back and punch his younger self in the face. It was just one of the many times he had hurt her.

He had chased after her. "I'm sorry. I didnae mean it. You're not an *eejit*."

He had nearly caught up with her when she turned around. He almost ran into her.

"But I am. I'm an *eejit* for having you as a friend." She gave his chest a half-hearted push, but her anger was already gone, and she started to smile.

"Now what's that?" Alex bent to look at the smile that threatened to bloom. But her lips looked so soft that he stopped wanting to tease her and wondered what kissing those lips would feel like.

"I see what you're trying to do, but it willnae work, Alexander MacDonell! I'm not one of your village girls who gets lost in your charms."

Alex came back to his senses, somewhat. "My village girls? Well, at least you find me charming." He indulged in a satisfied smirk.

Kenna had pounced on his back as she used to when they were children and wanted to wrestle. But they had grown too old for that. The sudden weight of her body threw him off balance, and they fell and rolled a short distance down the hill. Alex landed on top, looking at Kenna. She was no longer fighting but just looking at him with her gentle gray eyes and full, parted lips.

She wasn't the young girl she had seemed only hours before. Their eyes met, and they couldn't seem to move. Her body felt soft beneath his. The next moment, Alex rolled off her and angrily told her she was daft to think she could fight a grown man.

Kenna laughed. "A grown man! You might look a wee bit like a man, but you're stupid!"

"I was stupid to follow you here." Alex scrambled back up the ridge to go home.

"I was stupid to bring you!" she hollered after him.

SHE HAD to be in that clearing. Alex looked at the steep climb before him. After going as far as he could on horseback, he tethered his horse near the top and climbed on foot. He found her sitting in the cleft of the ridge, looking at her home.

"I didnae think you would remember this place," she said calmly.

A soft smile formed on his lips. "I remembered how angry you were."

"Hurt, not angry. You never understood the difference."

"Aye? Well, it's hard to perceive the distinction while you're pounding your fists on my chest."

Kenna turned and reluctantly smiled at the sight of his mischievous grin. "Life was simpler then. You'd annoy me, and I'd hit you." She shrugged and lifted her twinkling eyes up to meet his. But her cheer soon dissolved. "It's not simple anymore. And everyone's gone." She looked back at the farms and swallowed.

Alex sat beside her, at ease with the silence between them.

She said, "I ken that it wasnae your fault, and I'm sorry I blamed you."

He was quiet. "That farm is yours. I could not look

at that land and that cottage without seeing you in it."
Kenna turned away, but Alex lifted her chin with the
tips of his fingers. "Look at me, lass." Soft wisps of her
hair caught the sun like crimson silk as he peered into
her shimmering eyes. His gaze hardened. "I will never,
ever ask you to leave it."

So much had happened in the years since they had
been there. Each moment together, each person they
had both loved, and each sorrow they had suffered had
spun themselves into threads. Some had frayed, others
had broken, but the ones that remained twined their
two souls. As Alex gazed into Kenna's eyes, he saw the
strength with which those threads clung to them each,
and he knew that they could not be parted without
doing harm. He had seen too many people wounded
and slain—some in violent and horrible ways, some by
his own hand in battle—but he would not see Kenna
hurt anymore. Not by him. Not by anyone.

Kenna sank into his arms, and he cradled her head
on his shoulder.

Chapter 4

Words and Deeds

IN THE DAYS THAT FOLLOWED, KENNA STAYED CLOSE TO home, for it felt like her home again. Yet she would never feel rooted by the land anymore, for although her people had lived and died there, the ones who came after her would not. Even so, she was grateful to Alex for letting her stay in her home. But whenever she came to that thought, she wondered how much his wishes would matter if something happened to him and the land went to somebody else. The thought of anything happening to Alex drove her thoughts from the land.

Alex had been kind and attentive since that day on the ridge, but his kindness was no more than a friend and neighbor might offer. She was sure he felt guilty and had done what he could to make things right for her. That was all.

He came by every day to make sure she was well, and he wouldn't leave before fixing something that she had neglected since Roddy's death. Alex was a good friend. That she wished for more was the source of too much introspection that did her no good. He didn't have those feelings for her, and she had to accept it. That didn't stop her heart from skipping a beat when she heard someone approaching on horseback.

Mari called out in the crisp autumn air, and Kenna rushed outside to greet her. After leaving the horse in the byre with some water and hay, Kenna brought Mari inside the cottage to warm up by the fire.

"I'm afraid that I cannae stay long. The days have grown so short, and I promised Callum I would be home well before dark."

"Well, it's good to see you! I've missed having someone to talk to. I've stayed close to home this past week."

Mari looked at Kenna. "Well, that's why I'm here. I haven't seen you since the Glengarry spoke with you."

Kenna met Mari's concerned gaze and exhaled. "A few days after that, I went into the village. I dinnae ken how, but word does travel. Well, I heard someone say something about Alex… about Alex and me… that he was letting me stay in exchange for—well, you can finish the rest. It was vicious blether, and I haven't been back to the village since."

"I'd heard talk, and I worried," said Mari.

"*Och*, it's the same girls who used to tease me for playing with the boys. I just liked to run and fish and hunt. It's so much more fun than sitting about pushing needles through cloth. We were *bairns*. But when I grew older, they started to say things."

Mari said, "Nae doubt they were jealous to see you with those *braw* lads."

Kenna smiled. "Well, they were a fine lot. I forget that you knew them all too from their time in the lowlands."

"Oh, aye. Of course, my favorite was Callum."

"I should hope so!"

"He rescued me, along with my heart, and I've loved him since." Mari smiled with a faraway look in her eyes. "*Och*, those brawny soldiers from the Highlands. Duncan was so handsome with his deep-brown hair and brooding eyes. Charlie was all charm and mischief. And Hughie…" Mari paused then smiled. "Hughie, I'll have you know, was beginning to draw the ladies' attention from Charlie. You can only imagine how Charlie took that!"

With a laugh, Kenna said, "Good for Hughie! Charlie deserved to be put in his place."

"And then there's Alex…"

Kenna met her gaze. "Aye, well, he's been a good friend. That's all that he is to me, and I'm grateful for that."

Mari's brow creased as she pondered Kenna's reaction. "Alex speaks very well of you—and often—for someone who is just a good friend."

"I can assure you"—Kenna shook her head—"if it were anything more, I'd have noticed." She leaned back and sighed. "But it's not. And I'm getting used to it—well, I'm trying."

"I disagree. But I think he's troubled. Dinnae give up on him yet. Give him time."

"I have waited, but it's a lonely thing to wait for

something that will not ever happen. Now I'm here with my memories, and I miss hearing voices and life about me."

Mari thought for a moment. "The céilidh's in a sennight, and you, my friend, are coming. It will do you good to get out."

Kenna shook her head. "I've grown used being at home with the quiet—and the memories. I'm not sure that I'm ready to be around so many people again."

Mari looked almost stern. "Yes, you are. You've learned all those dances! It would be a great favor to me."

Kenna couldn't refuse her dear friend.

ALEX TOOK a drink from his tankard of ale then set it down with a satisfied grin. He took in the small tavern, its smoke-darkened walls, and the heavy oak tables. Nearly everyone who lived near the castle wound up there at some point. "'Tis like our days in the city, but without having to do the king's bidding."

Callum nodded. "It was worth it to meet my love. But the rest of the business I'd gladly forgo."

For a moment, neither spoke as they thought of the men they'd become and the men they had lost. Alex had no desire to speak of that time. Reliving it at night and waking in a sweat was enough. Those days would never leave him.

He shook off his mood. "Aye, 'tis good to be back."

Callum leaned forward conspiratorially. "Now, you'll come to our céilidh?"

Alex gave him a halfhearted grin.

Callum leveled him with his officer's look. "That wasnae a question. Mari's made it quite clear. You're to come, or you'll answer to her."

Alex laughed. "Well, in that case, I cannae miss it."

"I thought that would be your answer." Callum leaned back with a twinkle in his eye. "Your neighbor, Kenna, will be there."

As Callum said her name, a girl from the village plopped down beside Alex and sidled closer to him. "A céilidh?" She winked at Callum then slipped her arm under Alex's arms and snuggled against him.

Evading the subject, Callum said, "I was just saying to Alex that some music and dancing would liven this place."

Alex shut his eyes and exhaled then forced a polite smile for the young lady draped on his arm. "But 'tis our sorry fate that we have none at the moment."

Her eyes brightened. "I can sing while you dance with me." She sprang up and tugged at his arm, nearly losing her balance in the process.

Alex grabbed her arm to keep her on what he realized were unsteady feet. "Thank you, lass, but I'm not in the mood for dancing. There must be some other lad here with a yearning to dance."

She took offense and straightened. "Do you think I'd dance with just anyone, Alex MacDonell? It was you that I asked!" She leaned forward until she was close to his face. "But I guess you're too busy dancing with your neighbor girl, Kenna." The corners of her mouth turned up in a satisfied smile. "I suppose she must pay the rent somehow."

He lurched forward, but Callum clamped a hand on Alex's arm. Alex forced himself to appear almost calm, except for a muscle that twitched in his jaw. "You'd best hold your tongue, girl."

Callum took the young woman's hand and pressed a coin in it. "Go have a dram, and good night to you, lass."

Alex fumed. "*Glaikit eejit*. What was she blathering about?"

Callum said, "Well, I'd heard there was talk."

"From where?"

"Kenna told Mari."

Alex groaned. "So they've been saying such things to her too?"

"Aye."

"The poor lass." Alex curled his fingers into a fist. "There's nothing to be done about it. Anything I say or do would only make us look guilty in their wicked wee minds."

Callum cursed to himself. "I'd have looked into it sooner, but I feared it would just make it worse."

Alex glanced about the tavern. "Well, life must be dull for folk to make up lies for their own entertainment, the bastards."

"I'm sorry."

"Dinnae be sorry for me. 'Tis Kenna I worry about."

Callum studied Alex as he voiced his concern for Kenna.

Unable to shake his foul mood, Alex said, "Have you had enough of this place?"

"Aye." Callum gave some coin to the barkeep and

followed Alex outside. As they rode away, Callum said, "Never mind. In a week, they'll have something else to gossip about."

Alex made a guttural noise of disgust. "But not before they drag her name through the mud."

"And yours too, I'm afraid."

"I dinnae care about myself. I care about Kenna."

With a slow nod, the start of a smile showed in Callum's eyes. "Aye, well, we all care about Kenna."

THE NEXT TWENTY-FOUR hours found Callum's house in a flurry of activity. The women had had little to celebrate since the men had gone away, but Kenna's mourning was nearly over, the men were home, and there was peace among the MacDonells and their neighboring clans. It was time for everyone to set down their burdens and be merry before winter confined them to their homes.

Saturday night found Mari fussing with a stray strand of hair. While Callum donned his plaid, Mari smoothed her hands over her flat stomach and looked into the mirror. He came over to her and circled his arms about her waist and held her close. They had said all the words they could say.

Mari forced herself out of her mood. "I would enjoy seeing Kenna lighthearted again."

Callum pinned on his kilt brooch. "She's had a difficult time these past years. Her brother was all she had left. Roddy was under my command."

Mari touched Callum's cheek. "I didnae mean to bring up sad memories."

Callum said, "After we all left for battle, we promised to look after each other's families if anything happened to us, and I will keep that promise."

"I ken that you will."

Callum grasped Mari's shoulders. "If anything ever happens to me, I hope you'll continue to do the same."

"Of course." She searched his eyes then lowered her gaze and touched Callum's chest, hiding a swell of emotions. Regaining control, she caught sight of herself in the mirror. "*Och*! That one bit of hair!" Welcoming the distraction, she fussed with her hair. Strong arms circled her waist.

Callum buried his face in her neck. "You look bonny. In fact, I've a mind to keep you right here with me for the evening." He spun her around by the waist and made a good argument for staying.

But as his hands slipped from her shoulders to cup her breasts, Mari whispered, "Our guests will arrive soon."

With a deep, throaty sigh, he touched his lips to the satiny skin that rose in mounds above her stays. His lips brushed a path up her neck to her mouth. "When, exactly?"

Breathless, she whispered, "When what?"

Callum's mouth spread in a satisfied smile. "When will our guests arrive?" He didn't wait for an answer but gave her a long, thorough kiss.

Mari tightened her grip on his shoulders to steady

herself. "Would you have me greet our guests flushed and panting?"

"No, but I like you that way, so I'd best keep you here." Callum's face lit as he kissed her once more and released her.

With a sigh, Mari turned toward the mirror and saw her reflection. "*Och*! Look what you've done to my hair."

He came up behind her and looked over her shoulder into the mirror. "You look bonny." They gazed at each another's reflection, then Callum kissed Mari's temple. "I'm not a patient man. I'll expect to continue this later."

"It so happens that I've a notion to let a *braw* man have his way with me later this evening."

Callum lifted a brow above smoldering eyes.

With a wink, Mari said, "So if you see one, do let me know." She turned to leave but not too quickly to receive a swat on the behind.

Chapter 5

The Dance

THE FLOOR HUMMED FROM THE CONSTANT TAPPING AND shuffling of feet as plaids swung about from the dancing. Kenna watched, too apprehensive to let anyone close enough to ask her to dance. Alex MacDonell was nowhere to be seen—not that she had been looking. They were friends and no more. Snippets of words and phrases peppered the air as Kenna wended through the room. Two young men rose and vacated a pair of chairs. Kenna sat just as a pair of young women glided past, covertly pursuing the men. But the gentlemen found two other dance partners, so the young ladies lingered and chattered.

"Aye, my sister married a man from the village," said the first. "She couldnae manage the cattle on her own, and he had no land."

"Did she not love him?" said the other.

"That doesnae matter. Now they both have full bellies, a roof, and a peat fire to warm them."

Her friend pouted. "I could never do that."

"If you got hungry enough, you'd do worse than that."

"Worse? *Och*, no."

"Everyone has to have food and a warm place to sleep, but a body can survive without love."

The second young woman wasn't convinced, but the words stuck with Kenna. She was safe and secure for the time being, but who was to say that she would be tomorrow? She had lost too many people to trust that Alex would always be there to protect her. Even if she didn't lose her home, she had a farm to run all alone.

From time to time, Mari arrived with a young man in tow, whom she would promptly introduce to Kenna, then she would even more promptly disappear. Kenna conversed while she kept an ear tuned to the music. As it came to a close, she made an excuse to leave before any of the men could ask her to dance.

That strategy worked for the first two men, but then she found herself face-to-face with her neighbor, Niall Sanderson, a widower with unflagging persistence. He was tall and narrow, with a long face and strong chin. His brown hair was thin and neatly pulled back at the nape. He was quite pleasant looking, except for the fact that he never seemed truly to smile. His mouth would curl up on one side as though he wanted to smile but couldn't find anything quite compelling enough to catapult him to full amusement. He had five young children at home, which Kenna supposed must account for his lack of humor. Perhaps he was simply too tired. His attentive air, which some might call eager, advertised that he was in search of a bride. He almost literally pinned Kenna to the wall, at which point Kenna chose the lesser evil of dancing.

The next dance wasn't one she knew, a fact she wasn't aware of until the music commenced. The realization sank to the depths of her heart, which was pounding. She had only just opened her mouth to excuse herself with sincere and hasty apologies when Niall lunged forward, hooked her arm, and swung her around. She did her best, first to keep her feet near the floor, which was not always easy, and second to mimic the steps of the women around her. That might have worked had they not had to pivot and switch hands with their partners, then pivot again and take four steps forward and back. Kenna never quite caught on to what came after that.

Somewhere during one of the turns, she bumped into her partner and bounced back, only to step on the foot of the woman behind her. Gasps of surprise and displeasure soon followed as people collided. Niall managed to extricate Kenna from the chaos, and in that moment, she glanced up to see the alarmed face of Alex MacDonell. His eyes locked onto hers, and only after the full agony of the moment had run its course did she manage to look away.

Mr. Sanderson mercifully led her in another direction. Between apologies, Kenna pleaded to go outside for fresh air, which Mr. Sanderson took to include himself. Outside, it was dark enough to conceal her face, which she could only assume reflected the depth of her misery.

"There's more to life than dancing," he said.

Kenna turned toward him and couldn't help but

laugh through her embarrassment. "Oh, Mr. Sanderson, I truly hope so."

The humor in her words escaped him. At that point, she became aware that they were alone in the dark and that Mr. Sanderson was leaning closer. As the warmth of his breath brushed her lips, Kenna turned toward the house.

"Thank you, Mr. Sanderson. I'm quite refreshed now." She sprang to her feet and walked back to the house.

He caught up with her at the door. As she stepped inside, Alex eyed them sternly from a few feet away, and Kenna bristled. She didn't need his approval, and she needed his disapproval even less. So she turned to Mr. Sanderson, smiled warmly, and took his arm. He led her to a pair of chairs next to the wall.

By that time, Alex had found a dance partner and was crossing to his partner's place on the dance floor, which brought him in front of Kenna. He pivoted and was gone the next moment, but she couldn't avoid seeing him, for the dance kept bringing him back close to her. He seemed too absorbed in the dance and his partner to notice Kenna. Who was his dance partner? Kenna had certainly never seen her. Judging by her elegant gown, she came from finer stock than Kenna. Her gown of vivid blue silk brocade made Kenna's skirt and jacket look plain. The two danced with such ease, exchanging a word now and then. His smile lit not only his face but anyone near him. Including Kenna.

"I said, may I bring you some claret?"

Startled, Kenna turned to Mr. Sanderson and

nodded politely. He rose to go find some refreshments. As she watched him walk away, she wondered at his attentiveness to her. Although they were neighbors, they had talked little beyond the usual greetings and discussion of the weather. She couldn't escape the likelihood that he was not so much pursuing her as he was in search of a wife. But was that such a bad thing? He wanted the same things she did: a safe home and someone to share it with. She had heard it said that people could grow to love one another, but she had never believed it. He was pleasant looking and nice, but could she ever sit with him—and his five children —and feel the comfort of home? She felt a pang of longing. Could that be enough? Kenna shook her head, for she couldn't imagine it.

"Is something the matter?"

The rich baritone voice startled her. She looked at Alex. "I beg your pardon?"

"May I?" Without waiting for her answer, Alex sat beside her in Mr. Sanderson's chair. "You were frowning and shaking your head."

A wave of warmth filled her heart, reminding her of something she had not felt all evening. At the same time, it brought to life the aching loneliness she had tried to forget, not to mention reminding her of the look on his face when she had ruined the dance or his disapproval when she had returned from outside. She couldn't seem to break free from her warring emotions or of his power over her. "I—"

"Are you unwell?" He put the backs of his fingers against her flushed cheek.

His touch made it worse. "No, Alex, I'm fine." She

pulled back in what must have seemed like distress, for he promptly withdrew his hand.

"Is there a problem?" Mr. Sanderson stood beside them. He must have seen some of their exchange, for he looked as disturbed as Kenna, though for far different reasons.

Alex tossed a vexed look at him. "No." He searched Kenna's eyes until she looked at Mr. Sanderson. Alex quickly stood. With a nod, he said, "Excuse me," and left them.

Mr. Sanderson sat beside Kenna. "I must leave soon and get home to the children. I've a housekeeper watching them, but she's not been well this past week."

The best Kenna could offer was a polite smile and her hand. "It was lovely to see you again, Mr. Sanderson."

He held her hand just a moment too long. "I wonder... would you mind if I called on you?"

Kenna had not expected the question—at least not that evening. Still disconcerted from her encounter with Alex, she couldn't clear her head to compose a proper reply. Her mouth hung agape.

"Whom shall I ask for permission?"

He was clearly planning more than to call upon her. He intended to court her! They had only just met. She had thought they might come across one another at some point—a cordial conversation at market or perhaps visit over tea after that—but this was so much more! "I don't know. I didn't think—I'm sorry, Mr. Sanderson."

He smiled. "I would like it if you'd call me Niall." Her flustered state seemed to charm him, as if feelings for him might have caused it. "Shall I ask Mr. MacDonell?"

"Mr. MacDonell?" she said, thinking of Alex.

"Callum," he said, his brows furrowed.

"Oh." Too flustered to think, she glanced about—anywhere but at Mr. Sanderson—until she caught sight of Alex MacDonell. He looked directly at her then turned and went out of her sight.

"Kenna? May I call you that?"

She offered a smile and a rushed nod. "Please excuse me."

Mr. Sanderson found his way to Callum while Kenna walked to the kitchen. She wanted to run, but she forced herself to walk out the back door, where she sat on a bench. This wasn't what she had hoped for this evening. A gust blew the leaves on the ground, and a warm jacket slipped over her shoulders.

"You were shaking from the cold." Mr. Sanderson sat beside her.

"I thought you'd gone."

"I've upset you."

Kenna started to deny it.

"No, it's my fault. I've forgotten how to do this. I'm sorry."

"No, it's me. I don't know if I'm ready."

He leaned his arms on his knees, his hands touching at the fingertips. "Of course. You barely know me. We need not call it a courtship—not yet."

He smiled in such a kind way that Kenna thought perhaps, given time, she might learn to care for him enough to spend a lifetime of evenings beside a warm fire. There were all sorts of love, after all.

Mr. Sanderson seemed more content. "I'll have a word with Callum—not of a formal courtship, but I'd like to assure him that my intentions are honorable."

Even as Kenna nodded, she wondered what she was doing. The loss of her brother had left a void. Without realizing it, Sanderson had managed to find her weakness.

Mr. Sanderson stood. "Good evening."

"Oh, Mr. Sanderson, here—take your jacket."

"Not unless you come inside where it's warm."

Kenna acquiesced and went back inside. When they reached the hallway, she stopped and bade him good-night. His eyes shone as they swept over her face. He touched her shoulder and gave it a squeeze before leaving in search of his host. Kenna smiled, but it faded as he disappeared around a corner. At least he wouldn't make her heart ache the way Alex did.

As the hour grew late, many guests headed homeward. Kenna watched the remaining few couples dance, including Mari and Callum. It was time to retire, she decided. Mari had insisted that Kenna spend the night, so she had but a quick walk up the stairs. When she arrived at the top of the stairs, Alex was halfway down the hall. It was too late to avoid him.

"I thought you had gone." She didn't want her heart to surge with feelings for him, but she couldn't help or deny it.

"Listen," he said in that rich, quiet voice that soothed her soul.

Playing was the song he had sung while they practiced dancing together. Without a word, he took her hand, and they danced all alone in the hallway. With his sure hand, he guided her, and he quietly told her which step or direction came next. She fell into sync with him as they had when they practiced. The wall sconces glowed in rich amber as Kenna and Alex stepped and glided together. His body was strong and sure, and she found herself mirroring his confident warmth. For those brief minutes, Kenna was wholly content.

The music ended, and Alex gazed into her eyes. "Well done." He smiled and looked truly pleased— perhaps even proud.

She was lost in the depths of his gaze. "Thank you."

He seemed surprised, and his brow creased as he dismissed her thanks with a turn of his head.

Kenna said, "You made me feel like I could dance —just a little."

"And you can." He took her hands. It was as an encouraging gesture, but it made the world stop—at least their world. He studied her hands in his, and he let his thumb stroke her skin as he lifted his eyes to meet hers. A half smile formed on his lips. He said her name with wonder.

As she met his gaze, Kenna felt as though she could dance or do anything else with him, because he believed in her.

She didn't know when the music had stopped, but the musicians were packed up and bidding Callum good-bye at the foot of the stairs.

Callum called up, "Alex! Is that you? Dinnae forget that we're hunting tomorrow."

Alex gently let go of Kenna's hands. "I'll remember. But dinnae wake me too early." He whispered to Kenna, "Are you coming with us?"

Kenna shook her head. She didn't need to go hunting or anywhere else with him.

"Tomorrow then—after the hunting." He put his hand on the small of her back, and they walked down the hall.

He was staying the night. Tomorrow she would see the man she had promised herself not to love, but instead of regaining control of her heart, she was trying to remember what had prompted her to make such a promise. When they arrived at her door, Kenna thought from the way his eyes swept over her face to her lips that he might kiss her.

His eyes rose to meet hers. He squeezed her upper arm for an instant and stepped back. "So I will see you tomorrow?"

"I imagine you will."

His lips widened to a smile that warmed her. "Good night."

Kenna murmured good-night then turned and struggled with the door handle. Alex reached around her. She slipped her hand from under his, and he worked with the latch. She breathed in his scent and resisted the urge to lean back into the warmth of his chest. The latch lifted at last, and he pushed open the door. As she turned, her thanks came out in a breathless whisper. He nodded while his eyes bore through hers. She couldn't have looked away had she wanted to.

His lips parted, and he said simply, "Good night again."

She couldn't be sure whether she even answered him. Only well after he was gone did she close the door and lean back against it as her heart went from leaping to aching.

Chapter 6

Two Dreamers

AFTER HOURS OF SLEEPLESS TURMOIL, KENNA WAS sleeping at last when a man cried out. Kenna sat up. He cried out again. Kenna flew from her bed, pulled on her robe, and rushed to Alex's room across the hall.

She frantically rapped on the door. When he failed to answer, she called his name and rattled the latch. It was unlocked, so she opened the door and went inside. She heard Alex thrashing about, moaning and mumbling nonsense. His bedclothes rustled as he grew increasingly agitated.

"Alex! You're having a nightmare." She bumped into a chair and righted it before it fell over.

In sudden silence, Kenna moved her hands back and forth in the darkness, trying not to bump into something. A hand clamped about her wrist and thrust her facedown onto the bed. A cold blade touched her throat.

"Alex, please," she pleaded.

Just as quickly, the blade was gone and fell to the carpet with a dull thud. Alex gripped Kenna's shoulders. "Kenna?"

She could scarcely whisper an answer.

"What are you doing here?" He didn't sound like himself.

"You cried out. I thought you were hurt," Kenna spoke softly.

He loosened his grip on her shoulders.

"Alex, what ails you?"

Alex released his grip and stroked her shoulders. "I'm so sorry." He touched her face gently. "God's teeth, lass, I cannae even see your face in the darkness. You must think I've gone daft."

"No." She didn't think he was daft, but her heart raced from the fear she had felt at his hands.

Alex took her hand and brought it to his lips. "You'd best go now, lass." He guided her to her feet beside him.

His plaid brushed against her as he pulled it from a chair and wrapped it about him. Kenna took in a breath when she realized he had been fully nude and was only barely covered now.

"I'll see you back to your room." Alex took Kenna's hand and led her to the door.

Making certain to keep her out of sight behind him, he looked both ways down the hallway. All the sconces had been blown out hours ago. The pair stepped across the dark hallway to Kenna's bedroom. Alex opened the door for her.

"I'm so sorry I frightened you. It was good of you

to be worried about me." He lifted her hand and kissed it. Without another word, he returned to his room.

Kenna closed the door and let out the breath she had been holding. She tried to memorize every word, every touch, the feel of his fingers, and the power of his presence. As Kenna thought through each moment, her soaring heart imbued each word and act with significant meaning, but she knew that was of her own making. Alex had had a bad dream. He was grateful she woke him and sorry he had scared her. There was nothing more to it.

THE NEXT AFTERNOON, Alex rode home with Kenna. After helping her tend to her horse, he insisted upon walking her to her door.

"There's no need to escort me all the way to the door." Kenna smiled, but uncharacteristic shyness gripped her when her eyes met his.

"I'll not leave you out wandering alone."

The warmth in his eyes struck her so, it was all she could do to conceal its effect on her heart. "I did a good deal of wandering alone while you men were gone."

Regret darkened his eyes. "It grieves me to think of you all alone here."

She couldn't form the right words. The loss of her family was a sorrow that never quite left. At his mention of it, loneliness gripped her anew. Alex brushed wisps of hair from her cheek then rested his hand on her shoulder. The small gesture comforted her in a way she couldn't voice, yet she felt as though he understood.

Kenna forced her sad thoughts away and assumed a bright tone. "Come inside. You'll at least have some ale for your trouble."

"'Twas no trouble, but I will have that ale."

As they stepped out of the byre and rounded the corner, beating horse hooves sounded. A half-dozen British soldiers rode over the hill. Alex pulled Kenna back around the corner and shoved her against the stone wall of the byre. Dirk in hand, he pressed his body against hers to shield her.

"Alex—"

He covered her mouth with his hand until the soldiers had ridden past. His heart beat against her chest as he pinned her to the wall until they had disappeared over a hill. When they were gone, he pulled her into his arms and held her until his breathing grew steady.

"Alex, they're British soldiers. You fought with them." She tried not to show just how much he had alarmed her. Alex had never been one to be fearful.

He snapped, "They dinnae ken me, and you shouldnae trust them." He held her face and peered at her with fire in his eyes. "Dinnae ever let them see you here alone."

Frightened, Kenna shook her head, barely able to move within his tight grip. A rock from the wall ground into her back. "Alex, you're hurting me." As she searched his eyes, his softened.

He seemed to awaken as he stepped back. "Kenna." It was almost a question. He pulled her into his arms and cradled her head as his cheek brushed against hers. "I'm sorry. I was trying to protect you."

Confused, she assured him, "I know. It's all right. They're not looking for me, and they'll not look for Covenanters here in the Highlands."

Alex looked away, troubled.

Kenna hooked her arm in his. "Come, I'll get you something to drink."

Once inside, Alex got a peat fire blazing, then he sat in a worn wooden chair by the fire. He was himself again, which put Kenna at ease.

As she handed him a cup, the memory of her father sitting in that same chair came to mind. "It's good to see someone sitting there again." Kenna pulled up a stool and sat facing Alex.

"You don't mind?"

She smiled. "Father wouldnae have wanted it sitting empty. And you ken how fond he was of you."

Her words brought a warm light to Alex's eyes. In the firelight, the warmth of small moments shared between them and with her family brought her comfort. Yet, through the quiet moment of contentment, the troubling question could not be ignored.

Kenna mustered the courage to ask, "What happened, Alex?"

He looked at her as though he didn't understand, but she knew him too well not to see that he was evading her question.

"Just now—and last night."

His eyes sharpened before he regained his composure. "*Och*, that. I was worried about you. Just because they're in uniform doesnae mean they cannae harm you. Last night was only a dream—nothing to worry about." He flashed her the grin that never failed to charm ladies.

But his charm wasn't enough to distract Kenna. She knew him too well. "It seemed like a bit more than that." Kenna had had many dreams, some of them bad, but none that would have made her hold a blade to someone's neck. Without thinking, she touched her throat.

He met her doubtful gaze with a wounded look in his eyes. "I'm sorry I frightened you, lass. I've been living for months as a soldier—sometimes I awaken and forget that I'm home."

Kenna might have left it at that if he had not stared into the fire and brooded. "How often?"

"What?"

"How often do you have that dream?"

"Oh, I dinnae ken." His eyes flashed, but he stood and turned from her. "I'm not daft, if that's what you're thinking." He stepped away as though he couldn't stand in one place.

Stunned, Kenna said, "I thought nothing of the kind!"

He snapped, "I would never have hurt you!"

Kenna rose and went to him. "I know that." She touched his shoulder, but he kept his face turned from her.

"Dinnae hover about me. I'll be fine." An angry edge to his voice sharpened his words. She started to walk away, but Alex grasped her arm. "Kenna, I'm sorry."

Looking down, she said softly, "I was worried is all. I dinnae mean to hover."

"I know." He loosened his hold and gazed at her with eyes brimming with pain. He looked as though he might say something more, but instead, he glanced toward the door. "There's no need to worry, lass. I'm home now, and I'll be better in time."

Kenna nodded despite being unconvinced.

He kissed her forehead. "I'll stop by tomorrow."

He rode away while she watched through the window.

THE MORNING that followed brought a damp autumn chill. By late afternoon, a mist hung in the air and obscured any view beyond Kenna's farm. She was in the byre, mucking the stables, when she heard a familiar voice in the doorway. "Good day, Mistress McCowan."

"Mr. Sanderson, what a surprise!" Kenna worked to replace her initial dismay with a smile. She knew she should have sounded more welcoming.

Before she could speak again, Niall Sanderson walked in and took the rake from her hands. "If you'll allow me—"

"Please, there's no need."

"It would give me pleasure to help you."

He was already at work. Short of arguing with him, Kenna could do nothing except watch. After a minute or two, during which Mr. Sanderson looked over and smiled, Kenna made an excuse to leave.

"I'll go make us some tea."

He stopped long enough to watch her disappear through the doorway. With the tea made, Kenna put some oatcakes on a plate then added some peat to the fire. A knock sounded at the door.

"Come in," she called as she wiped her hands on her apron. "Alex!"

He walked in, smiling. "You look surprised. I told you that I would come by today."

"Aye, so you did."

He looked at the oatcakes. "There's too much here for you to eat on your own."

"But she isnae alone." Niall Sanderson walked in and gave Alex a narrow-eyed look. "Is that your horse down by the stream?"

Alex folded his arms. "Aye, it is."

"You had best tend to it before it wanders off."

Alex met Sanderson's flinty look. "He'll not do that." He turned to Kenna. "I can see that you're busy. I'll be on my way."

Mr. Sanderson opened the door for Alex.

"Alex—" As she said it, she could think of nothing to add that would ease the awkward tension without offending one or the other. She followed him to the door. "Mr. Sanderson surprised me with a visit to help with some chores. Wasn't that nice of him?"

Alex grunted in agreement.

Ignoring him, Sanderson turned his attention to Kenna. "I thought we'd agreed that you'd call me Niall."

He smiled at her with a familiarity that made Kenna look away to find Alex clenching his jaw. She wished she could tell Alex how she felt, but what good would that do? He didn't share her feelings.

"Alex, won't you stay for some tea?" she asked.

"I've never cared much for tea." With a terse nod, he left.

Chapter 7

Broken Dreams

It was nearly dark before Sanderson left. Two hours had passed—two hours of talking about her life and her farm. He had asked her to walk him about and point out the boundaries and the head count of her cattle and other livestock. He also talked of his own land and holdings and gave a description of each of his children.

After he left, Kenna watched him disappear from view. As she did, all she saw was the look on Alex's face when he had walked away hours before. Kenna mulled it over for a moment, then strode to the byre, saddled her horse, and rode toward Alex's house.

When he answered the door, his tousled sandy hair fell freely over his forehead. He pushed back his untamed hair and offered a crooked smile. "Kenna, my darlin', come in."

He gestured for her to enter with an unsteady flourish that confirmed Kenna's suspicions. "You're drunk."

His only response was a broad grin and a hand on her waist to guide her inside while he closed the door.

Kenna planted her feet close to the door. "I can see this isn't a good time."

Alex chuckled. "We both suffer from that." Seeing Kenna's confused frown, Alex elaborated. "From poor timing. Why, only today I had the poor timing to interrupt your little love tryst."

"My what?" Anger roiled within her. "How dare you imply—"

"Quite easily, actually."

Kenna slapped him hard. Had he not been drunk, he would have seen it coming and blocked it. Instead, he just put a hand to his cheek.

The only trace of his smile was the gleam in his eyes. "I hope he's ready for you. You're a spirited lass."

Kenna glared. "And a proper one too. I'll not have you ruin my character."

As he walked over to the table to pour more whisky into his cup, he muttered, "*Och*, but I'd enjoy ruining you."

"What did you say?"

"You're doing a fine job of that on your own." His anger softened to pain as he looked into her eyes.

"Ruining my character? *Och*, you're too drunk to ken what you're saying."

"Oh, I'm drunk—I'll not argue that point. But I ken what I'm saying."

Her contempt was weakened by the pain his words brought her. "Say all that you like, but you'll say it alone. I'm leaving."

His hand clamped about her wrist. "You shouldnae

be inviting men to your house with you there all alone. 'Tis not right."

"I didnae invite him. He arrived. What was I to do, turn him away?"

"Aye!"

Kenna exhaled, exasperated. "I see. So the next time you come calling, I'll turn you out too!"

"I'm different."

Bitterness rose within her. "I suppose that you are, since there's nothing between us."

Alex shot her a sharp look. "I'm an old family friend."

Kenna lifted her chin and nodded. "Oh, aye, and what a good friend you are. Why, look at the fine job you did today of protecting me."

Alex stiffened and gripped Kenna's shoulders. "What are you saying? Has he hurt you?"

Kenna dismissed his concern with a laugh. "No, he hasnae hurt me. The only man who has hurt me is you!" She regretted the words as they flew from her mouth. "What I mean is, with your accusations."

"Do you truly believe he has feelings for you?"

"Is that so hard to believe?"

"No." Sorrow tinged his voice.

She scowled. "I suppose I should thank you for that."

"But why Sanderson? Any fool could see that you feel nothing for him."

She glared at him. "No, not any fool. You dinnae know how I feel—nor did you ever."

Alex sank wearily into a chair and shut his eyes. "Aye, I'm a fool. I'll not argue that point."

It was all Kenna could do not to shake her head at the miserable sight he presented. Instead, she took pity and pulled a chair close beside him. "Alex, what's happened to you? I've never seen you like this."

He gazed into her eyes, at which point Kenna feared she had drawn her chair too close to his. His green eyes met hers with a staggering force, searching her until her chest pounded in response. His unguarded expression was almost childlike. The drink had broken down his defenses.

"I've never felt like this, lass."

"Like what?"

Alex looked away. "Like everything I've ever longed for is within reach. I can see it, but it will never be mine."

Kenna ached with the impulse to tell him that she would be his if he'd ask her. "What are you saying?"

With a weak chuckle, he said, "I dinnae ken. Look at me. I'm too drunk to make sense."

"Are you?" she said quietly.

He leveled as sober a gaze as she'd seen since arriving. "You said so yourself."

"So I did."

"Would you do something for me?"

"Aye." She leaned forward and resisted the urge to smooth his hair into order. She knew she would not stop there, for her fingers would trace his cheekbones and full lips. Then she would want to taste him.

Alex said, "Would you add some peat to the fire?"

Kenna leaned back and exhaled. "Aye."

She felt his gaze follow her as she bent over and tended the fire, but she pretended not to notice. When she returned to her seat, a long silence followed. She waited until she could stand it no more. "I should go."

He covered her folded hands with his large, battle-scarred hand, and he lifted his stormy green eyes to meet hers. Kenna feared her heart would burst from the effect of that look.

"Is Sanderson good to you?"

Kenna frowned. "Good to me? Aye, I suppose."

"Then you have my blessing."

Kenna wanted to slap him again. "Do I now? Well, good. I would hate to have a cup of tea with Mr. Sanderson without your blessing!"

Alex stared at the fire. "He's in love with you."

Kenna looked at the window. Darkness had fallen outside. Inside, only the fire lit the room, making the space seem smaller. "There's a difference between being in love and wanting a wife."

"And what do you want?"

You. For years, she had loved him, but for years she had known that to tell him so would risk any friendship they had. So she did as she always had done—she skirted the truth. "I would like to be loved—as anyone would."

His hand tightened about hers. "You will always be loved."

She knew the warm glow of the fire caught the tears in her eyes. When the silence grew too long to bear, Kenna looked over to find him asleep. She let her eyes sweep over him in a way she could rarely allow. The tiny lines on his forehead and about his eyes warned of a strain that he kept to himself. She was tempted to trace the strong lines of his nose and his jaw. The beginnings of a beard stippled his jawline and framed lips she would touch with her own if only she dared. She drank in the sight of his sturdy shoulders and chest that narrowed to a lean waist. From there, he was covered in thick folds of plaid, leaving her to imagine the rest.

Kenna slipped her hand from beneath Alex's. After she banked the fire, she quietly stepped toward the door.

"I'll not send you into the night all alone." Alex rose.

"I thought you were asleep!" Kenna felt him draw near but did not turn around. "I know every bit of bracken and grass between here and my home."

"So do I, and I'll see you through all of it."

She turned to find that he was much closer than she had realized. "Really, it's not necessary. I—"

He put his fingers on her lips, and it silenced them both. Neither moved until their halting breaths steadied, and his fingertips slid from her mouth. He reached past her and unlatched the door, and they left the warmth of the house behind them.

"Coffee?" Alex asked as Kenna poured him a cup.

"It was a gift." Kenna avoided his questioning eyes.

"From Sanderson?"

Kenna turned away, suddenly busy rearranging items in the cupboard. "Aye, it was."

"I've a mind not to drink it," he said.

"I've a mind to force you. It'll bring you back to

your senses. I cannae have you falling asleep on your horse."

"*Och*, that horse knows the way home better than I."

Kenna smiled. "I'm sure he does. But will he put you back on his back if you fall?" Kenna sat with a cup of her own.

Alex laughed. "You needn't worry. I've been far drunker than this."

Kenna grinned. "I've nae doubt about that. Still, I'll worry."

He leaned forward. "Why, Mistress McCowan, I'm flattered." He peered into her eyes with the mischievous glint that charmed all the lasses.

His crooked smile finished the job on her heart, which fluttered beyond her control. She wouldn't let him see his effect upon her. "Dinnae flatter yourself. I would worry about any old oaf drunk as you."

He leaned back and laughed. "Aye, well if I don't flatter myself, who will? Surely not Mistress Kenna McCowan."

She had always loved how his laugh seemed to spring from deep inside, true and unguarded. It was one of the few times he was simply himself.

"And what makes you smile like that, Kenna Henna?" He had caught her grinning, but invoking her childhood nickname snapped her out of her dream. He smirked in that boyish way that used to infuriate her, before she grew old enough to be charmed by it.

"*Och*, dinnae start on me, Alexander Gander."

But before she had finished, he was making hen noises to tease her as he had when they were children.

Kenna gave an admonishing shake of her head. "Have you forgotten what that used to earn you?" As a child, he'd made a hen pecking motion until she grabbed hold of his nose and gave it a firm twist.

But when she reached for him, he grasped her wrist and drew her closer until she felt the sweet warmth of his breath on her lips.

He said, "That was before I grew taller and stronger than you."

His triumphant smile faded, as did hers. Their eyes met, and neither seemed able to move. A question formed as his gaze pierced hers.

Her hand twitched in his tight grip. He looked down and released her in an instant. "I'm sorry. I dinnae ken—"

Ignoring the truth that had passed unspoken between them, she said, "We're no longer children." What began as a smile faded as she watched his troubled gaze fix on the fire.

"No, I ken that."

Kenna tried to make light of the uncomfortable silence. "Alex, you take me too seriously."

But when he turned his dark look upon her, she saw it was more than her words that troubled him. There was something in his eyes she had not seen before.

He turned back toward the flames. "I wish I could go back to when life was clear and I knew where I was going. Now, I feel lost." He glanced at her. "I'm not daft." His eyes darted back to the fire.

"I ken well that I'm here, but inside—in my mind—I am back there in the lowlands, following orders that I know are wrong. They go against everything I believe. But I swore to serve my clan and my country. To do that, I became someone else. Now I've returned to the land that I love, but the man I once was is lost out there somewhere. I cannae manage to find the way home."

Kenna searched his face, but it held little emotion. He appeared as lost as he claimed, and that troubled her. "What does Callum say?"

"Callum? Why would I tell him about this?"

"Because he went through it too."

"Not through this. He was gone by the time Bloody Clavers took charge of us."

"But surely he understands what it's like," she said.

"That may be so, but I'll not talk to him about it."

"And why not?"

"Why? Because he would see that I'm weak," Alex said.

"Weak? Now you are sounding daft! You're anything but weak."

He peered at her. "How can you look and see only the good?"

"Because I know you." She looked at her hands. He seemed to look through her eyes to her heart, and she couldn't let him see what was there.

"You see the man I would be, but I am not that man."

"But you are. You're a good man, and you're kind."

Alex rolled his eyes.

Kenna went on. "And you're brave, and you're strong."

"Oh, my body is strong enough, but a man of strong character wouldnae have done the things I did."

"I'm sure you did as you were ordered, for that was your duty."

"Aye, that makes me a good soldier—but not a good man." Alex turned hollow eyes to her. "I am not the same man you remember."

While she wanted to protest, she remembered the feel of his dirk at her throat. The man who woke from that nightmare was indeed not the Alex she knew. He was troubled but would not ease his burden by seeking help from others. Instead, he buried his anguish. With as much whisky as he'd had that evening, there might be no better time to get him to talk.

"Have you told anyone about the dreams?"

He grimaced. "I told you. No one else need know. It was only a dream."

Kenna leaned toward him. "I think it was more."

"Do you? And what gives you the right to think anything at all about me?"

Kenna leaned back and stared at her coffee. "Nothing."

He laid his sturdy hand on hers and stroked the tips of her fingers with his. "I'm sorry, lass. I dinnae ken why you put up with me." With a gentle pat, he withdrew his hand.

"Because you are my friend, and I am yours." Kenna's eyes flitted up to meet his, and she forced a cross look. "And if I didn't, who else would put up with your foul moods?"

That drew a fleeting smile from Alex. "Aye, true enough. I'm no good to anyone now."

She said what a friend ought to say, but she feared he was right. "I dinnae ken what you mean when you talk so."

"*Och*, hen. What I mean is—" He looked at her with a weary warmth that made her heart ache. "You deserve all that's good in the world, and I'd give it to you if I could. But the truth is I have nothing to give— not to you, not to anybody."

"You gave me back my home, and that is my world." She felt false as she said it, for she knew that she wanted much more. She wanted him.

The sorrow in his eyes struck a blow to her heart. Alex's mouth spread into a smile, and he shook his head slowly. "There, you see? You see only the good."

"I see the truth, which is what good friends do."

Alex's eyes filled with emotion. "You give of your-self, which is not always easy. All I've done is let you live on land that I didn't expect to own and of which I had no need. There was no sacrifice in that."

"You say that because you're a good man. I accepted your help. Now you must accept mine."

He turned away, and his voice broke. "You dinnae have what I need."

It was a harsh blow, but Kenna took it with barely a wince. Alex had always been the one in control. Strong and sure, his thoughts were always his own. But turned inward as he was, no one could reach him now.

Still, she couldn't be silent. "No one will ever offer you what you need if you refuse to let anyone see what it is."

He hunched over, elbows on knees.

"Alex?" Kenna went to his chair and put her hand on his shoulder.

He turned, and his arms flew about her as he hid his face in her waist. She smoothed her hands over his hair. He got up so quickly that, startled, she stepped back. He muttered an apology and stormed out of the house, leaving her staring at the door that he had just slammed. Kenna sank into the chair, tears trailing down her cheek. For a long while, she sat by the fire as sparks rose and burned out. Kenna flinched when the door opened again.

Alex strode back in and pulled up a chair beside her. "I will tell you what a good man I am." His eyes were rimmed with red as he watched the fire. His voice was quiet and deep. "It wasn't a dream. It was real. 'Tis the memory of it that now haunts my dreams."

Alex shifted his weight in the chair. "I left home to do something noble for my clan and my king. At first, I suppose that it was. But that was before Bloody Clavers. He came by the name honestly. We were out on patrol, and we rode through a thick mist to a small farm in the lowlands. A family lived there—husband, wife, and their children—not soldiers. We went to their home and roused them from their sleep in the hours before morning. They were simple, God-fearing people who wanted to worship in their own way. The farmer and his wife were known Covenanters who had been seen at a recent conventicle—a secret kirk service outside."

Alex turned to Kenna with rue in his eyes. "I didnae want you to know this, because you will hate me. But I cannot live with the lying—not to you. It eats at me, and you deserve more. All I have in the world to give you is the truth, and it's all you'll want from me after tonight."

His eyes were tender and thoughtful, just as Kenna imagined love might look. "You're talking nonsense." She wished he were joking, but she knew he was not.

Alex's gaze swept from her hair to her lips, then he turned and went on. "The other day, I'd been up all night. In the morning, I awoke from one of my dreams, and I went to the window." He glanced over and met her eyes. "I picked up my pistol."

Kenna's eyes widened, but she did her best to keep her emotions in check.

Alex said, "I looked out over the field, and I saw you walking by. You were carrying a basket, and the sun caught your hair. It was like strands of fire. You looked…" He smiled. "And I thought of the loved ones you've buried." His voice broke. He barely got out the rest. "I was afraid that if I pulled the trigger, you'd be the one to find me."

"Alex." She didn't try to hide her alarm as she reached to him, but he lifted his palm to stop her.

"I couldnae do that to you." Clearing his throat, he said, "Bloody Clavers led us to that farm, and he went inside and brought everyone out of the house. The mother and children—there were four, all young—all standing together. You'd think they would cry, but they didnae. They watched us with blank stares. Clavers gave the orders. I pulled the husband away from his wife and his children. I had done it before, but those men had then spoken the Oath of Abjuration, so we could let them go. That's all they needed to do. They were just words. But the husband looked at his wife, and she nodded, and they both refused. All they needed to do was promise not to take up arms against the king and to renounce the Covenant. But they would not.

"Clavers told them the penalty for refusing, but they would not say those words. Clavers ordered me to shoot him.

"'But the children,' I told him.

"'It will be a good lesson to them.'

"I said, 'You cannae mean—'

"'Shoot him.'

"I told the man to say the oath, but as I spoke, Clavers went to the wife, hooked his arm about her waist, and held his pistol to her head. He told me to fire on the husband, or he'd shoot the wife. That farmer looked at me, and he nodded for me to do it. He was sparing his wife. So I did it. I shot him." Alex leaned back in his chair. "Then Clavers shot her."

Kenna touched his hand, but he gently pushed her away and said, "What kind of man does that?"

"A man who is weak and unworthy."

Alex said, "Aye, that's what I am."

Kenna leaned forward. "That's not what I meant. I meant Clavers!"

"What kind of man follows orders he knows are morally wrong? When is it time to refuse? Surely that was the time. But I didnae refuse. I did as I was ordered."

Kenna's heart ached for the lives ruined and lost and the spirit broken before her. "But what could you have done? Clavers would have shot her, then him, and then you, I imagine."

"Aye."

"If you had shot Clavers, then the other soldiers would have been bound to execute you for treason."

Alex nodded. "I've thought through it so many times."

"You had no choice," Kenna insisted.

"But I did, and I made the wrong one."

Kenna shook her head and refused to believe him.

"The same wrongs would have been done, but I would not have been the one to do them. I would have died doing right. Instead, I lived because I shot and killed a man in front of his wife and his four young children."

"So the dreams—"

"They haunt me. That is my penance." He walked to the door.

"Alex, wait."

"I wanted you to know the truth about me. You deserve at least that." He stared at the door but made no move to leave. When he spoke again, he sounded distant and forced. "Sanderson will ask you to marry him soon. Tell him yes." He looked at her then left.

Chapter 8

Safe and Secure

KENNA DID NOT CRY THAT NIGHT, NOR DID SHE THE next day. He had taken the air from her lungs, and she couldn't get past the shock of it. She knew he had never been hers and she had suffered no loss. What right had she to behave as though Alex had broken her heart? If anything, he had done the kind thing by making it clear they had no future. She reminded herself of that again and again. Women spent their lives without love. So would she.

For a week, she got up every morning and went on with her day—with her life—because that was what one did. But one morning, as she carried a pail of milk from the byre, she heard a horse, and she knew it was his. She set down the pail and pressed her back to the cold stone wall inside the byre. After he'd ridden past, she felt tears on her cheeks. She slid to the ground and wept.

ON A GRAY MIDAFTERNOON, Kenna sat by the fire. Rain drizzled, and an occasional drop fell in through the chimney and sputtered against a peat ember. She drew her *airisaid* around her shoulders and went on with her knitting. She had never especially enjoyed knitting, but it kept her distracted from the thoughts that kept forcing themselves upon her.

Outside, a horse rode up and stopped. She couldn't pretend not to be home, for the fire had already given her presence away, so with a sigh, she braced herself. She knew she would have to face Alex at some point. Perhaps getting it over with would be better than prolonging her dread.

Kenna opened the door. "Mr. Sanderson!" From the warm light in his eyes, she realized he had taken her surprise to be pleasure at seeing him.

"Niall," he corrected.

"Niall." Kenna forced a polite smile.

He was dressed in a finely made doublet with silver buttons, and the plaid he wore only to Mass. Only then did she realize it was Sunday.

He stood in the doorway and looked at her, concerned. "When I didn't see you at Mass, I grew worried. Are you unwell?"

"No, I—well, yes, I've been feeling ill. Won't you come in?" she asked to distract him from inquiring further into her health.

Niall didn't mind talking, which was fine with Kenna, for it relieved her of responsibility for maintaining the conversation. But as the afternoon wore on, Kenna grew weary of his narrations of all he had done to his farm. He seemed to know more about his livestock than his own children—except to assure her of how obedient they were. They were spending the day with a neighbor, which freed him to be with her into the evening.

"How nice," Kenna said, hoping her smile didn't look as weak as it felt.

"Is that sun I see coming in through the cracks in the doorway?" Without waiting for an answer, Niall walked over and flung open the door. The sun had indeed come out from the clouds it had hidden behind. "We must go riding." It was not a question.

So they went, for Niall enjoyed making decisions, and Kenna felt too hopeless to argue. She recalled Alex's last words to her. If Alex didn't want her, then one loveless marriage was the same as another. She wondered what sort of life she would have, married to Niall. With his penchant for making decisions, would she just fade away until she was like another piece of furniture to him: present, useful, and silent? So that was what Alex thought would be best for her?

Niall seemed to enjoy riding with her. He took a particular interest in her farm, nodding as though making note of her land and livestock. At one point, he surprised her by offering an estimate of her earnings with astonishing accuracy. He had a good head for business, which spoke well for his future prospects. But every time Kenna tried to imagine a future with Niall, she found herself filled with despair. Wasn't that to be expected? She'd lost hope of love, so what was left to look forward to?

As she pondered her prospects, they arrived at the road and met Alex MacDonell. There was no escaping him. He drew closer and stopped facing Kenna and Niall. Niall was amiable as always, and Alex was more polite than she ever had seen him—so much so that she felt like a stranger.

"The sun's come out, after all," Niall said with cheer.

"So it has," Alex answered, looking politely past her.

Kenna wanted to cry out, "And you've broken my heart!" But she just nodded.

Niall said, "'Tis a fine day, after all."

Alex said, "Aye," with a nod. For the first time, he let his gaze stray to Kenna. Although his expression revealed no emotion, his gaze pierced hers.

Oblivious to the thick veil of silence that had descended upon them, Niall said, "Where do your travels take you on this day?"

Alex tore his eyes from Kenna. "I beg your pardon?"

"Your travels. Where do they take you?"

Alex nodded. "I'm off to see Mr. and Mrs. MacDonell."

"Ah, very good, very good. Send our warm regards, will you?"

"I will." With a curt nod, Alex rode off.

MARI SAW Alex comfortably settled in a chair by the fireplace and excused herself to go speak with the cook.

Alex stared at the fire until Callum said, "Well? What is it?"

Torn from his thoughts, Alex looked up absently. "Sorry?"

"You've been brooding ever since you got here. What is it?"

Alex shook his head and turned back to the fire. "'Tis nothing worth speaking about."

"Aye, I can see that." Callum studied Alex for a moment then casually said, "Have you seen Kenna lately?"

A dark look flashed over Alex's face. "Kenna? Aye."

"And when was that?"

"Just now."

Callum watched Alex closely. "Ah, I see. Where was this encounter?"

"On the road near her home. Why would you ask about her?" Alex's eyes darted angrily about the room.

"Because you're in love with her." Callum looked squarely at Alex.

"You're daft."

Callum said, "Maybe so, but I'm right, and you ken it."

Alex cursed.

"Mari saw it when you danced, but once she called my attention to it, I didnae ken how I'd missed it. It's true, is it not?"

Alex pushed some stray bits of hair from his brow then sank back into his chair and glanced at Callum. Despite his annoyance, he said, "Aye."

"Then what's wrong with you, man? The girl's been besotted with you for years."

Alex seemed genuinely surprised.

Callum nodded. "When I saw you two dancing, I thought that you'd come to your senses at last."

"I think that's when I knew it." But it was not love that showed on Alex's face.

"You dinnae look very happy about it."

Callum and Alex had been through many battles together and found themselves close to death more than once. The raw trust between them had formed a bond that would be there for life.

Alex said, "I'm not the same man I was. After you and Mari left, things changed."

Callum said, "Aye, I've heard stories about Bloody Clavers."

"They're true. I thought I'd left it behind, but it weighs on me." Alex's eyes moistened, but he kept his emotions in check.

"How so?" asked Callum.

"I betrayed my own sense of what's right and wrong."

"Why?"

Alex looked at Callum. "Because I was ordered to."

"You followed orders as a soldier should."

"And when should a soldier stop and say that his orders are wrong? There must come a time." Alex stared in earnest at Callum.

Callum said, "There are things I regret, but I know that I did my best to serve my laird and my king."

"So did I, but—"

"Then accept it and put it behind you."

"I cannae. What I did as a soldier has destroyed who I am as a man. 'Tis a powerful thing to have done something so wrong that it cannot be made right no matter what you do."

Mari returned but hesitated at the doorway.

Callum said, "That lass over there made me whole."

Alex glanced fondly at Mari. "The woman's a saint for putting up with you." He managed a smile, but it was gone just as quickly as it came.

Callum said, "Love has a healing power all its own."

"It has not healed me." Alex fixed his dark gaze on the fire.

"It's her love for you that can bring you back home." Callum gazed at Mari, who stood behind his chair with her hands resting upon it. "Have you thought about the future—a future with Kenna?"

Alex started to speak but stopped to regain his composure. "I'm broken. I've nothing to give her."

Mari said, "Yourself. That's all that she wants."

"She deserves more."

"Does she?" Callum was firm and direct. "Such as what—Niall Sanderson? Is that whom she deserves?"

"He will keep her safe and secure. She needs that."

Mari said, "And is that what you need?" When he did not reply, she pressed further. "Is that what you long for—to be safe and secure?"

"What I long for, I can't have."

"Why not? What stands in your way?" Callum leaned forward.

Alex leaped up and pounded his fist on the mantel. "Stay out of it, Callum!"

Mari said gently, "What if it were Kenna who felt as you do? If she were hurting, would you leave her in pain and go marry a woman you felt no love for?"

The mere thought enraged Alex too much to answer.

Mari fixed her soft eyes on Alex. "Well then, how do you expect her to do that to you?"

"I expect her to be happy—or at least content— and she'll never be either with me."

Mari said, "She'd be with you. That alone would make her far happier than Niall Sanderson ever could."

Alex looked at her. "I told her to marry him."

Callum's mouth was agape. "My God, you're a fool."

"Callum!" Mari gave him a cross look then put her hand on Callum's shoulder. "Give her a chance."

"A chance? To gamble on me? What if she loses?" He leaned on the mantel and stared at the peat embers. "I've ruined my own life. I'll not ruin hers."

"What if you lose her?" Mari walked up behind Alex and put her hand on his shoulder.

He spun around and yelled, "Stop!"

Callum reached for Mari's arm and pulled her back before he stepped between them. "Dinnae talk to my wife that way."

Mari said, "It's all right, Callum."

"No, it isnae right, and I'm sorry." Alex looked from one to the other. "I'm sorry. Can you not see I'm of no use to anyone?"

Mari said, "I see that there's something wrong, and you willnae let anyone close enough to help you."

Alex cast a troubled look at her. "I'm not ready."

Callum said, "Well, you'd better get ready, for Sanderson is, and he's wasted no time in making it known."

All the anger Alex had felt moments earlier was gone, and a calm settled upon him. "I want Kenna to be happy."

Mari said, "She needs you for that."

"Perhaps I might have made her happy once, but 'tis too late now."

Mari stepped toward Alex, but Callum held her back. She said, "There was a time, as you well know, when I thought I'd lost Callum. But I knew he loved me, and I loved him with a vehemence that brought out strength I didn't know I had. Let love be your strength until you've got yours back."

For a moment, Alex was too moved to speak. "Mari, you're an angel, and a strong one at that." He gazed at her fondly. "I ken that you mean, but there's no help for it." With a shake of his head, Alex left.

Chapter 9

The Promise

ALEX RODE HOME, UNABLE TO GET HIS MIND OFF WHAT Callum and Mari had said. He believed them with every bit of logic his mind possessed, but his heart had been damaged by what he had seen and done. He could hardly feel anything anymore—except when he looked at Kenna. If he were still capable of love, he would love her beyond measure. She deserved that, but he could not give it to her. Love had seeped into his heart and opened a wound. Now the pain he had buried away was exposed. As much as he loved her, he did not feel it as he should.

He saw that she felt something for him, but what sort of man was he for her to love and be proud of? If Mari was right and Kenna loved him, he had already hurt her enough. How much more would he hurt her by yoking her to a broken man? Anything he had once had to give her was gone. After honor and moral integrity were lost, what of any value was left in a man?

Had he not done her a favor by urging her toward Niall Sanderson? He had little doubt that Sanderson wanted to marry her. But thoughts of her marrying Sanderson—or anyone else—stabbed his scarred heart. Alex may as well have been mortally wounded in battle, for he felt his life draining from him. Only one thing reminded him that he was alive, and that love hurt him until he cried out in despair. The sound that came out was a choked-off, guttural sob. He would never get past his guilt and shame, so he had pushed her away. He had hurt her to spare her a worse pain.

Even so, Callum and Mari were at least partially right. He owed Kenna the truth, and it might ease her sorrow. He might be too lost to find his way back to her, but he would at least tell her the truth. That would help her to understand why he couldn't be with her, even though he loved her and would love only her for the rest of his life.

Alex urged his horse on. It was nearly dark, but he and his horse knew the path. He had made his decision. He would give her the truth and, with it, his love, though he could not take her love in return. At least she would have that.

Forgive me for breaking your heart. I do love you. He said aloud, "I love you." He said it again. The more that he said it, the more he felt life creep back into his soul. His desire to tell her grew stronger, and with it came hope that he might feel again. Perhaps that could be a beginning. In time, love might drive out his pain.

His plaid flew behind him as he rode to her farm. Once there, he dismounted and bounded toward the cottage. Before he reached the door, Kenna slipped outside.

She spoke in hushed tones. "Alex? Has something happened?"

"No. Yes, I suppose that it has." He couldn't take his eyes from her.

Kenna's brow creased with confusion. "What is it? Is it Mari or Callum?"

"No. *Och*, I've been an *eejit*. But I've come to my senses."

With each moment, she appeared more distressed. "Alex, we can talk in the morning."

He took hold of her shoulders. "Aye, but first I must tell you one thing. I've not been honest with you. Kenna, the truth is, I love you."

Alex had imagined a number of ways that she might react to hearing those words, but her grief-stricken moan was not one. He touched her cheek, and she flinched. A sigh followed soon after, and that sigh drew him to her. Without thinking, he brushed strands of hair from her brow and bent to kiss her. Her lips parted as he drew closer, and he kissed her with all the love he had tried to hide.

The door opened behind her. Kenna's hand flew to cover her mouth as she turned quickly to face Niall Sanderson. He stood in the doorway, blocking the light. As Alex watched Kenna's shrinking reaction to Niall, irritation with Sanderson quickly replaced the love he felt.

Sanderson was at Kenna's side in an instant. "I didnae ken you had company. Why did you not invite him inside?"

Alex opened his mouth to speak, but Kenna spoke first. "He just stopped by on his way home, but he cannae stay."

Alex nodded then said to Kenna, "I'll see you in the morning."

Upon hearing that, Sanderson took hold of Kenna's arm and said to Alex, "You'll do no such thing."

Alex leveled a cool stare at Sanderson. "She will do as she pleases, regardless of what you or I wish her to do." He turned back to Kenna with a questioning look.

Sanderson said, "I'll not have you entertaining men by yourself."

Kenna turned back to Sanderson. "Entertaining men? We're old friends!" *Friends who kiss.*

Alex frowned at her, but she looked so dismayed that he put his own feelings aside. Something was troubling Kenna, and that troubled Alex.

Sanderson stood behind Kenna, gripping her shoulders. "Kenna has other plans in the morning."

"Does she?" Alex leveled a glare at him as he tamped down his anger. He turned to Kenna. "I'll come by in the morning."

Sanderson said, "No, you'll not come calling here anytime soon."

Alex shot a sharp look at Sanderson. "I believe that is for Kenna to decide." He looked into her doleful eyes. "'Tis your home, hen."

Kenna's face softened, for they both knew that by law, it was Alex's home. By rights, he could cast them both out.

Alex gave her an encouraging look. "You dinnae answer to him."

Sanderson said, "But she does."

Alex bristled.

"She will soon be my wife." Sanderson smiled triumphantly at Alex's obvious shock. "I just asked her, and Mistress McCowan has agreed."

The battle was done. Sanderson had wielded the better weapon, and its blow landed squarely on its target. Alex opened his mouth to speak, but no words came out. He could only look at Kenna, whose stunned expression confirmed it.

"When I last saw you—" Color drained from her face.

He managed a nod but could neither speak nor tear himself free of her resigned gaze. When he could bear it no longer, he forced out false words of congratulations and left.

AT DAWN, Kenna knocked on Alex's door. When she got no answer, she went to the byre and saw that his horse was there. She returned to his door and knocked again, calling his name. When the door opened, a housemaid answered and told her that he was not at home. Kenna nodded, bereft, and walked back down the lane lined with hedgerows. She didn't see Alex watching from the second-floor window.

ALEX LEFT for Fort William the following day. When Kenna asked about him, Mari told her that he had some business to attend to that would keep him there for weeks.

Kenna gave up on her knitting and let it rest in her lap. "Weeks? Surely he'll come home before that."

Mari's eyes softened with sympathy. "I imagine he'll come home when he's ready—or able."

Kenna nodded, resigned. "After the wedding, I suppose." She sighed. "I asked Niall to release me from my promise to marry him."

Mari broke the rhythm of her knitting but resumed. "And what did he say?"

"We're still betrothed, as you see."

"Oh, Kenna. Even knowing how you feel?"

"He does not know how I feel, nor will anyone else. He reminded me that I have made a promise, which is binding under the law."

Mari's glanced up. "Under the law?"

Kenna nodded. "There was no more to say after that. I saw no point in fighting a battle I cannae win."

Mari abandoned her knitting to a basket on the floor. "Niall's not thinking clearly. I'm told that he's not been the same since his wife died."

Kenna spoke with little emotion. "No, and that's why he wants a clean home with fresh bread and a mother to care for his children. But he doesnae want me."

"Has he told you that?"

"No, but it doesnae feel like love."

Mari quietly said, "Perhaps that has more to do with how you feel."

Kenna couldn't disagree. "I cannae help how I feel, for I've always loved Alex. But when he told me to marry Niall, I was so hurt. Then I was angry. So when Niall asked, I said yes. I'd lost Alex, so what did it matter who I married? I'll never forgive him for that— or myself."

Mari said, "But you must. He was trying to spare you."

Kenna's eyes filled with tears. "So you've told me. But, you see, he has spared us both now, for I'll never be happy without him."

Mari squeezed Kenna's hand briefly.

Kenna's eyes shimmered with unshed tears. "Now two hearts are broken, and two lives are ruined." Kenna took a deep, bracing breath. "I must put love away and not speak of it ever again."

Chapter 10

The Solicitor

ALEX SAT IN A SMALL CORNER BOOTH OF A FORT William tavern with a whisky in hand. He had done little else since he'd arrived. What began in early evenings as warm thoughts and remembered desire turned to remembered mistakes, relived one after the other then started over.

As candlelight flickered through his amber-liquid-filled glass, a young woman slid into the booth with a swish of fabric. Her brown hair was swept back at the sides, and the rest hung, silken and straight, down her back. A few strands escaped to brush her sun-reddened cheeks. "I've seen you here before, and you're always alone."

Alex met her inquisitive gaze with a smirk. "So are you."

With her brow furrowed, she looked down and blushed.

Alex studied her. She was pretty enough through her soiled face, but her round eyes seemed to see everything as if for the first time, making her either too young or too innocent to be seeking his company. "How old are you, lassie?"

She sat up straighter, indignant. "Old enough."

"Old enough for what?" Alex started to laugh, but he saw he'd upset her, so he stifled the urge.

"To be married." She cast her eyes downward.

"Oh, married, are you? And where might your husband be?" He couldn't hold back the smile any longer.

"I said I was old enough to be married. I didnae say that I was."

Intrigued, Alex nodded, conceding the error in his assumption.

She smiled, but it was forced. "I thought you might like to talk for a bit."

"Talk? Well, that's one word for it." He looked at her plainly.

The young woman's eyes widened, but she lifted her chin. "You seemed lonely. I thought you'd like company."

"And now I have it." He studied her. "How long have you been in Fort William?"

"I dinnae ken. A few days, perhaps." Her eyes met his, but instead of seeming seductive, she simply looked lost.

Alex knew that look well, for it reflected his own state of mind. "What's your name?"

"Rose."

"'Tis a pretty name."

"Thank you." She smiled and nervously smoothed out the edge of her worn cuff.

When the silence grew too long, Alex said, "What brings you to Fort William?"

The question appeared to strike a chord, for her eyes flickered with pain before she averted them. After a steadying breath, she looked at him. "Work."

"And where are you staying?" he asked her.

Flustered, she averted her eyes and said, "I'll stay in your room if you'll pay me." She met his eyes boldly for a few seconds before returning to fidgeting with her sleeve.

Alex put his hand over both of hers. "I'll pay you to eat, for I can only guess you've not had a full meal in days."

Her eyes widened but were still tinged with unease.

"Dinnae *fash*, lass. I've no interest in bedding you."

"Why? Am I not good enough for you?"

He was astonished to see that her feelings were hurt. "*Och*, lass. 'Tis not that at all."

"I ken I'm no beauty—"

"No, you're a mess, truth be told." He clamped his hand over hers when she started to leave. "I'm sure, underneath all that dirt, there's a pretty face to be seen. But you'd not make a very good whore."

She angrily fought to pull her hand from his grip.

"And even if I thought that you would be, I willnae be your first."

She scoffed unconvincingly. "My first?"

"Aye, lass." He peered into her eyes, and she let down the facade.

Alex loosened his grip and stroked her hand gently. Something about her was so forlorn that it moved him. Whatever her reasons, she was as miserable as he was.

She had come to Fort William to escape and only found a life worse than the one she had undoubtedly left.

For the next half hour or so, he watched her devour a heaping pile of neeps and a Scotch pie filled with mutton. She ate with such a voracious enthusiasm that he couldn't help but smile as he ordered more food. When her hunger was sated and spending the night with him was well out of the question, she spoke more freely.

"So you've run away from home," Alex said.

She reluctantly nodded. "My parents wanted me to marry a man that they'd chosen. I refused, and they told me I didnae have a choice. It was settled."

"So you proved to them that it was not settled at all."

"Aye." She smiled, but it faded.

"You'd rather sell your body than marry a man you dinnae love?"

She shook her head. "I never thought I would even consider it, but I couldnae get work. No one will hire me without a reference from my kirk. The weather is growing cold, and I didnae ken what I would do. I saw you, and you seemed kinder than most, and I was so hungry and tired." Her tears caught the light from the wall sconce. "When I left home, I didnae ken it would be like this."

"The world's a hard place to be on your own with no money."

She looked at him with such sadness that he took her hand. "Is this what you want—a life like this?"

"No, but I've no choice."

"Go home, Rose."

"So I can sell myself to one man rather than many? Is that so much better?"

"Is he such a bad man?" Alex asked.

"No, but he's not a man I'll ever be able to love."

During his soldiering days in Edinburgh, Alex and his friends had spent their fair share of nights with doxies. They'd seen how such women suffered ill treatment from men.

"Look about the room, lass. Is this the life you want?" Alex asked.

The pub had filled up with people since she'd sat down with him. At the bar was a man with a beard and greasy hair. He held a mug of ale with hands darkened with grime and jagged fingernails black at the tips from the dirt underneath. He caught Rose looking at him and grinned knowingly at her. From the next booth came the sound of a slap. A woman stood, holding her face. She turned to leave, and a man yanked her back and hit her again. A few tables over, a woman traced a line along her décolletage and lifted her eyes to a well-dressed, round-bellied man. He said something into her ear as he slid his hand from her shoulder to grasp her breast. A moment later, they climbed the stairs and disappeared into one of the rooms. Rose looked away and wiped her eyes before succumbing to the tears just under the surface.

Alex said gruffly, "*Och*, that's enough of that, lassie. No tears before we've had our dessert. Let us finish our meal and talk about getting you back to your home. Would you like that?"

Rose smiled, and to Alex's surprise, so did he.

ROSE'S HOME was half a day's ride from Fort William, which suited him well. He was waiting for his solicitor to draw up some papers and taking Rose home would offer a diversion from drinking himself free of thoughts about Kenna. As they rode, Alex tried to prepare her for what might await her.

"Oh, I ken that my parents will be very angry." She fought back tears.

"If you were my daughter, I'd be furious with you. I'd also be glad to have you home safe."

"Well, I'm not your daughter."

"No, but you could be—well, perhaps my younger sister."

"I doubt that my parents will be so forgiving," she said.

"Give them time. In the meanwhile, you're still better off at home."

"I hope so. But I wish I didnae have to marry some old man of their choosing."

"Well, you may get your wish, for your groom will not likely appreciate your having left," Alex said.

"No, I don't imagine he will, but I didnae ken what else to do."

"Some will think the worst, so you'd best toughen up to prepare for what people will say. Whatever happens, hold your head high. You'll be the only one to believe that you've done no wrong while you were away."

Rose sighed. "Oh, aye, I ken it. But I'm tired of talking about it."

Alex gave her a gentle smile. "I suppose there's not much more to say on the matter."

Rose said, "So why did you run away?"

Alex laughed. "Me?"

"Oh, you cannae fool me." Rose glanced at him. "I knew it the first time I saw those sad eyes. It's why I chose you. And you're also not too horribly ugly." She fought back a smile.

"Oh? Well, I thank you for that." Alex smiled. He had thought he was no longer able to smile, but the stranger had managed to get his mind off his troubles. Helping her had somehow brought him out of the miserable place he had dwelled in for weeks.

Rose had cheered up as well, and she wouldn't relent. "So who was she?"

"And why must there be a she?" Alex said with a grimace.

"Men don't show their feelings unless they're quite bad, and that usually means it's a woman."

"It was much more than that," Alex said somberly.

Rose looked over her shoulder at him. "But there was a woman?"

"Well, if you must know——"

"I must."

"There was."

"I knew it!" she cried in triumph.

Alex arched an eyebrow. "You're very proud of yourself, aren't you?"

"Aye, but I'm also sorry to be right."

"Dinnae be. If I'm sad, I've only myself to blame for it."

Rose said, "What did you do that was so terribly wrong?"

Alex looked into the distance, ignoring the question.

"I think you should stop blaming yourself." Rose turned as much as she could from her seat in front of him.

Alex smiled at her unfounded confidence. "And why is that?"

"Because only a kind man would do what you're doing for me. So I know that whatever has happened, you're still a good man."

"Your logic is flawed," he said with a chuckle.

"I dinnae ken about logic, but I ken that I'm right."

"You're wrong, but I'm in no mood to argue."

"I'm wrong? So it's unkind of you to bring me home?" she asked.

"I dinnae say that."

"And kind people dinnae deserve to be happy?"

"I dinnae say that, either." He smirked.

"So what you're saying is that you are kind, and you deserve to be happy." She smiled.

"Very well, lass. You win. Henceforth, I shall only be happy."

"Good, then 'tis settled." Rose lifted her chin and gazed ahead, pleased with herself.

At midday, they stopped at the top of a ridge.

Rose pointed at a croft in the glen. "That's my home. I can walk back from here." When Alex protested, she said, "*Och*, no. If they saw you, they truly would think the worst."

"Aye, I suppose you're right. But I'll wait until I ken that you're safe at home." Alex helped her dismount, and they stood at the top of the mountain together.

Rose extended her hand. "Thank you."

He shook her hand. "Good-bye, Rose." He smiled but was unexpectedly seized with affection. "If you have any trouble, I'll be in Fort William for the next few days."

Rose gazed into his eyes then rose to her tiptoes and kissed his cheek. She turned just as quickly and said over her shoulder, "Good-bye, Alex MacDonell."

He left his horse grazing out of sight and sat by a tree and watched until Rose's father caught sight of her. Rose ran into his arms, and her mother ran out of the croft to join them.

As Alex rode back to Fort William, he began to believe that, like Rose, he could get through what was before him. With the ease that so often came with youth, she had simply let go of the past and moved forward. Perhaps he could learn from that. Or was it even simpler—had the mere act of helping another brought him out of his miserable state? He could only be sure of one thing: somewhere between there and Fort William, he had begun to discover the power of forgiveness and hope.

Chapter 11

The Battlefield

THE AUTUMN DAYS GREW SHORTER, WHICH MADE Niall's visits with Kenna grow shorter as well, for he left before dark every day. As the wedding approached, he grew confident, making plans for them. All that remained was to wed her, and that would come soon. They had posted the banns, and they would be married by the end of the month.

With Kenna's parents gone, Mari and Callum took on the role of bride's parents and invited the village to their home for a show of presents a week before the wedding. Guests presented gifts, which were then displayed on a large table, and the dancing began. As if forcing away the cold weather outside, people's spirits soared, helped by a plentiful supply of whisky and ale. A cold gust blew into the room as a late guest arrived. He received an especially boisterous welcome, which drew Kenna's attention from her conversation with Niall.

From the crowd, Alex emerged with a gift. Mari

seemed to appear out of nowhere to lead him to the table of gifts. Niall pressed his hand to Kenna's back to guide her along. Rather than be bothered by Alex's sudden appearance, Niall seemed to welcome the chance to gloat. She was his, and he had nothing further to prove. By the time they reached the gift table, Callum had joined them.

Alex was as courteous to Niall as he needed to be, and he kept his emotions in check, despite not having seen Kenna for weeks. He held out a disc-shaped object wrapped in an ivory silk cloth. Around it was a gray satin ribbon, tied into a bow. His eyes softened as they swept from the ribbon to her matching gray eyes. Kenna untied the bow to reveal a silver platter with a folded up piece of parchment upon it. When she lifted her eyes to Alex, he gave an encouraging nod, so Kenna unfolded and read the parchment.

When she was done, she looked at him, stunned. "What is this?"

Alex quietly said, "The land is yours now."

"What land?" asked Niall with genuine interest.

"Mine?" Her tears caught the light.

Knowing what his gift meant to her, Alex met her eyes for only a moment. He glanced away before he revealed how much it meant to him as well. "This document conveys it to you. It is yours to use as you will."

"My home." The words caught in her throat. It was the most precious gift anyone could have given her, and he knew it.

The room may as well have vanished as they stared at one another. Had he spoken, he would have shared everything on his mind and his heart. But he knew he could never do that, so he chose to say nothing.

Niall broke the silence. "But that farm was yours already."

Kenna shook her head, barely reacting as Niall took the document and read it.

He said, "It will be mine soon enough."

"Aye, 'tis true that a wife cannae hold property except through her husband," said Alex. "Unless it's a trust."

Sanderson said, "What sort of blather is this?"

Alex barely moved as he eyed Niall. "The land is now held in trust for Mistress McCowan. Any conveyance—or use, for that matter—would have to go through the trustee." Alex looked straight into Sanderson's glaring eyes. "I am the trustee."

Kenna glanced at the guests, who were beginning to notice the tension between the two men. Kenna whispered, "Niall, please."

Sanderson moved closer to Alex and lowered his voice. "A fine wedding gift this is, you bastard."

Alex said, "Oh, but there's something for you. The silver platter is yours." His mouth twitched a bit at the corner.

Sanderson's eyes flashed, but he held back his anger. When he finished glaring at Alex, he turned to Kenna. "You knew about this all along."

Kenna lifted her chin. "I knew nothing of the kind."

"Perhaps not the trust, but you knew you didnae own the land you lived on. Did you never think to tell me?"

"No. You never asked, and since I've never owned it, I didnae think it worth mentioning."

Sanderson sneered, "You didnae think? Are you daft or just stupid?"

"That's enough!" Alex stepped between them and guided Kenna behind him.

Meanwhile, curious guests gathered around them. Alex glanced about then locked his icy eyes on Sanderson's, as though daring him to make the first move. Several MacDonell clansmen put hands to their dirks.

Callum stepped forward. "Think what you're doing. Do you really want to discuss this here and now?"

Sanderson looked about then lowered his voice. "No, but we will speak again."

Alex said, "I imagine we will."

Sanderson turned to Mari and Callum and spoke up so the guests could all hear. "Please excuse me. I must go home to my children. Good evening." He offered his arm for Kenna to leave with him. When she averted her eyes and pretended not to see, he spoke with a quiet edge to his voice. "Mistress McCowan, I'll escort you home now."

Mari interjected, "I've asked Kenna to stay. We've some wedding matters to talk over."

He stared at her, his nostrils flaring, and nodded politely. "I see. Well, then, I bid you farewell." He took Kenna's hand and pressed his lips to it, then lifted his blazing eyes to meet hers. Turning to Callum, Niall said, "I will see myself out."

After they watched Sanderson walk through the

door, Callum announced to the crowd, "Nervous groom," and laughed.

The guests joined in with jokes of their own and resumed celebrating. Mari discreetly whisked Kenna through the kitchen and up the back stairs to her room.

Callum pulled Alex aside. "Do you ken what you're doing?"

Alex met Callum's eyes. "Not entirely, no."

"Your plan sounds brilliant, so far."

Alex wasn't fazed. "Well, it's better than standing by and watching him marry her."

"And what makes you so sure he won't marry her now?"

"I'm not. All I ken is that he cannae." Alex started toward the stairs, but Callum grabbed his arm.

"You're not going up there." Callum stood firm and held Alex in his steely gaze. "Keep your distance before you disgrace the poor lass. Do you not ken how many will see if you go to her now?"

"I'll go up the back stairs."

"Oh, aye, so the servants can gossip."

Alex turned away, defeated. "You dinnae ken how I hate when you're right."

"Aye, well, someone must be, and tonight you're far from it." Callum raised an eyebrow and clapped his hand on Alex's shoulder. "Let's go into the study." Once there, Callum poured two whiskies and set the bottle before them. "Tell me what's happened."

Alex emptied his cup and poured another. "There isnae much to tell. While I was in Fort William, I met someone."

"Someone?" Callum raised an eyebrow.

"Aye, someone who helped me look beyond myself to imagine a future."

Callum said, "A future with another man's bride?"

"He doesnae deserve her."

"So it falls to you to remedy that?"

"I love her."

Callum's brow arched. "I could tell. So could everyone else."

With a sheepish grin, Alex said, "I dinnae care."

"Well, you should care—for her sake."

Alex leaned back and stared at his whisky. "I never intended to make such a scene. But once we stood face-to-face, with him acting like he owned her, I couldnae help it." Callum said nothing, but Alex felt his disapproval. "Do you not remember how you were with Mari?"

Callum's eyes softened at the memory.

Alex said, grinning, "I remember a man wildly in love who barged into a Covenanter kirk service and rode off with a pretty young lass. That made a rather large scene, as I recall."

Callum's brows drew together. "That was different."

"Oh, aye—because it was you." Alex's mouth quirked up at the corner. "It was love. And we stood by you."

"I will stand by you—and that includes not letting you do something foolish."

Alex's aspect darkened. "When I first came home from the lowlands and saw her, everything changed. We would not be the same as we were, and I knew it."

"That might have been a good time to tell her. Could you not see how she felt about you?"

Alex shook his head. "No. I didnae ken how I felt —or even if I did. I was in no position to plan a future. I had nothing left for her. The only thing that felt good and right was making her happy. But I knew—or I thought—that being with her would just drag her down into the dark pit I'd fallen into. Letting her go was the one good thing I could do, but then seeing her pain made me want to protect her. Since then, I've started to feel again."

Callum poured another drink and leaned back.

Alex went on. "But I was too late. In the same instant, we knew we were deeply in love, and we knew that we'd lost one another."

Callum studied his friend. "What happened in Fort William?"

"I went to see the solicitor to take ownership of the land I'd inherited. But for the most part, I drank. I felt sorry for myself. Then I did something for someone who needed help. It was a small act, but for the first time since I'd come home, I saw something beyond my own pain. I began to think of how Kenna must feel, and I thought of her married to Sanderson. She'd be leaving her home. I didnae care what the deed said— that land was hers, the one thing she had left. I had the power to give it to her, but I wasnae about to let Sanderson take it from her. So I found a way to give it to her without letting Sanderson have it. Even if she never goes to his home, she'll know that hers is her own, and it's waiting for her."

"Like you?"

Alex took the blow like the soldier he was. "Aye. Well, there's nothing I can do about that, is there? I would want her no matter what happened."

"And you think that the land will change things?"

"It'll change things for her, for she now has her home. But to be truthful, I hope he'll not want her now that he knows he cannot have her land. I suppose I'm a fool for wishing so."

"You'll notice I've not contradicted that point," Callum said dryly.

Alex was too deep in his thoughts to bother with Callum's remark. "He doesnae love her. Seeing him with her just now made that clearer than ever. He only wants her for her land."

Callum's amusement faded. "I'd like to agree, but I've seen no sign of it."

"You will. By tomorrow, he'll realize he's lost the land he wanted, and then he'll release her from her promise." Alex set down his cup. "There it is. That's the plan you were asking for. Now may I see her?"

"No." Callum leaned back in his chair, resolute.

Alex stood and leaned over the desk, barely containing his fury. "She's not your prisoner."

"No, she's my guest—as are you—and I'll ask you to respect that."

Alex glared but returned to his seat.

Callum was quiet but firm. "People willnae look kindly upon you stealing her from him, and that will hurt her."

Alex looked away while he reined in his anger. "Not as much as living with him will."

"Perhaps, but what you hope for will come at a price only Kenna can pay."

Alex's eyes closed as if by doing so, he could keep out the truth. Then he went to the window to hide how deeply Callum's words had struck him, for he couldn't disagree. For a long while, Alex stared at the wind scattering the leaves over the ground. When he felt sure he had bridled his feelings enough to speak calmly, he walked back to Callum and sat. "What would you have done if this were Mari? You must have felt this way about her."

"Aye."

"So what do I do?" Alex turned away, scowling to hide his despair.

Callum leaned back and exhaled. "Are you sure that she doesnae want him?"

"How can I be? I've not seen her in weeks."

"I'll ask Mari to invite her to stay here, and— assuming she agrees—we'll let Sanderson simmer. When he looks past his pride, perhaps we can help him see that he's better without her. But I'll not do a thing until I'm convinced of her wishes."

Alex looked at Callum. "When I was away, it all seemed so clear."

Callum's brow furrowed. "Sanderson is a simple farmer who thought he had his life laid out before him. Now he finds himself face-to-face with a formidable man, both in stature and strength. He's too proud to acknowledge the threat you pose to his future, as well as his pride."

Alex shook his head slowly. "If he knew how defeated I've been these past weeks, any fear he might have about me would be put to rest. Muscular strength is of no use with a spirit that's broken."

"My friend, you underestimate yourself."

Alex shook his head.

Callum leaned forward on his elbows. "For very different reasons, I do ken what you're feeling. I have been nearly broken." Seeing Alex's doubt, Callum nodded. "Aye. When I was in prison, I did my best to be strong for Mari's sake. Duncan must have suspected the truth, for when I was transported, he signed on for the voyage to help me. That act and his presence gave me the strength I lacked. After my prison ship crashed, I wondered whether I would make it home to Mari. But help always came when I needed it most. I tell you this so you will let others help you."

"But all that you did, all that happened, came from doing what was right. I have not earned such good fortune," Alex said.

"How long have we been friends? I know you. Your faith in yourself, and your faith in what's good in the world, has been shaken. But I know you'll find your way back, just as I did. I also know that you may not be able to do it alone."

"How can I ask for help?"

"You'll not need to," Callum said. "I've not forgotten what you and the lads did for Mari when I was away. You looked after her like family, and I'll do the same for Kenna—and for you, as well."

All Alex could do was to choke back raw emotion.

"We've been through too much. We are friends, and although it may be harder to accept help than to give it, that is what you must do—as my friend."

Chapter 12

Between Hope and Despair

WHEN ALL THE GUESTS HAD EITHER GONE OR TUCKED in for the night, Alex sat alone in Callum's study. He set down a half-finished whisky and stared out the window. The dim light of dawn glowed through the dense fog. He loved Kenna. What Alex had to confront was whether he loved her more than his desire to be with her. Would he be able to do what was best for her if it didn't include him?

Alex rose from his chair and walked down the hallway. He paused outside the room where the dancing had been. Inside, Callum and Mari danced slowly without music. With a pang of envy, Alex went upstairs to the room he always stayed in when visiting. Across the hallway was Kenna's guest room. He looked down the hall to make sure no one would see, then he tapped on her door and said her name softly.

The door opened. There Kenna stood in her white muslin shift, clutching an arisaid about her. Her dark red hair tumbled loosely over her shoulders. Whatever he had thought he would say now escaped him.

She whispered, "What is it?"

"May I come in?"

"No, you know better than to ask that."

"You're angry." The look in her eyes made him ache, so he let his eyes drift to her hand. It was beautifully shaped, but her slender fingers were callused from farmwork.

Softly, she asked, "Why did you do it?"

"How could I not?" He let himself look into her eyes, knowing that Kenna would see everything in his heart.

She looked furtively down the hallway. "It was a generous gift, and I thank you for it."

Alex shook his head slightly to dismiss it.

"You ken what it meant to me," she said.

"I do. It gave me great pleasure to do it."

"But you ken just as well what it meant to Niall. 'Tis a cruel game that you're playing." She lifted her eyes to meet his.

He had misjudged her expression. There was no anger—only the tacit acceptance of pain. Alex knew that feeling well. Footsteps mounted the stairs as a soft laugh drifted upward.

Kenna tightened her grip on the door. "It's Callum and Mari. Go before they see you here."

"Let me in. Please, I must talk to you."

"No. You cannae!"

"Kenna, I love you."

She shut her eyes as though that would keep the effect of his words from her heart. "Dinnae say that."

"I must see you," he whispered.

"So you can break my heart all over again?"

Alex bent down, nearly touching his forehead to hers. Scarcely able to breathe, Kenna glanced toward the stairs.

Alex whispered, "Once. Meet me once."

The footsteps mounted the stairs. Alex drew closer, unable to stop.

Before his lips met hers, she pressed her hand against his chest and whispered, "At the bent oak at dawn."

Alex caught one last glimpse of her before Kenna closed her door. He closed his and slid the latch into place just as Callum and Mari walked by.

THE GRASS and leaves seemed to shiver as the wind blew over the hill where the bent oak stood, old and gnarled. Alex paced underneath. Since well before dawn, he had waited, convinced he was mad to dream of a future with Kenna. After the things he and his fellow soldiers had done, he had no right to hope for anything good, let alone love. Now he straddled a line between hope and despair and felt poised to fall back where he justly belonged. Then he spied Kenna riding toward him. The wind caught her arisaid, and it billowed behind her. The sight made his heart swell.

When she arrived, he reached up to help her dismount, and she said, "No, thank you. I can manage myself."

Of course she could. She rode as well as any man,

and better than some. But his offer wasn't about riding. It was about his longing to put his hands on her waist, to touch her and hold her against him. And it was about her making sure that he didn't do that.

Still breathless, Kenna said little while she tethered her horse beside Alex's. That task done, she turned. "I've barely slept. My better judgment told me not to come here."

"But you did, and I'm glad." His eyes swept past her cheeks, flushed with color, to her long, slender neck. He saw the strong girl she once was, with a wildness he had thought couldn't be contained. But now she was a meek shadow of who she had been and should be again.

"Dinnae be. You'll not want to hear what I have to say."

"Kenna, what has Sanderson done to you? Where's the spirited girl I once knew?" He put his hands on her shoulders to draw her into his arms, but she swatted him away.

"What has Sanderson done? It was you! You broke my spirit when you broke my heart!"

"*Och*, lass, I ken that I've made a mess of it all."

"Aye, that you have," she said bitterly, stepping away.

"I love you!" What more was there to say?

She stopped. Without facing him, she said, "Do you know how long I longed to hear you say that?" Alex drew a breath, but Kenna shook her head and went on. "But all you did was to push me away."

"I was a fool. I was not myself. I—"

She turned to face him. "I tried to understand, but how could I?"

"You did nothing wrong. I was—something happened to me while I was away."

Kenna eyed him with mistrust that cut him to the core. He stepped toward her, but she stepped back with the look of a cornered animal.

"Then you returned just in time for the wedding—just when I thought my heart had grown cold. That was the cruelest part."

Alex wanted to hold her until her pain and his went away.

"I could have gone on as I was, but you made me feel again," she said.

"Why did you do it?"

Kenna stared in disbelief. "Why?"

"You dinnae love him! So why did you promise yourself to him?"

"Because you told me to!"

"That's no reason to ruin your life."

"I had no life left. The only person I'd ever wanted did not love me." She glared at him. "So I did it because you'd hurt me. I wanted to hate you, but the truth is it wasn't your fault. I was to blame, for I trusted my heart without knowing that you'd keep it safe. I hated myself, and I was angry with you. My life was already over when Niall asked me to marry him."

The sharp stab of guilt was nearly more than Alex could bear. Alex reached for the tree trunk and leaned against it to steady himself. He could say nothing to absolve himself. She was right to despise him. He had wounded her deeply, and himself in the process. But he felt compelled, nonetheless, to give her the truth.

In a low voice, he said, "When I came home, I couldnae live with what I'd done. When I told you about it, you were so kind and trusting. Part of me was drawn to you. God's wounds, I wanted to lose myself in you! But you came too close, and the wound was too fresh. I was wrong to do it, but I couldnae help myself. I needed to shield myself from the pain. I'm a warrior. I dinnae ken anything but to fight and defend."

Kenna leaned her back against the oak and shut her eyes.

Alex said, "You forced me to feel. I didnae ken until I went away that I could still feel. I knew I'd hurt you." He brushed his knuckles over her cheek, but she flinched away from him. Alex continued, "I knew I'd lost you, but I had to do something. The land was the one thing I could do that wouldnae hurt you."

She turned toward him. "It was good and kind, but it hurt just the same."

"I dinnae seek anything in return. It was—and is—yours."

For the first time, her face softened as she gazed into his eyes. "I know. That was what hurt. There was something in your eyes when I looked up from reading that document." Her words caught in her throat. "It was love, and I knew it was too late."

Alex pulled her into his arms.

She struggled against him. "No! You've no right to do this!"

"I know." Alex loosened his hold but could not let go.

Kenna pulled free. "What makes you think you can come back and have me like nothing has happened?"

"I cannae think anymore." He brushed his fingers to her bare neck and chin.

Kenna tilted her head back. His breath warmed her earlobe and neck. Kenna spun around, threw her arms about his neck, and clung to him.

Her silken hair brushed his lips as he told her, "I'm so sorry."

She leaned into his embrace. Moments passed as they held one another, both mired in grief. Holding her face, he kissed her with the force of his desire.

Between kisses, he whispered, "I love you."

"We can't," she protested, making no move to be free of his arms. "I'm promised to him."

"No, you're mine." The next instant, his mouth was on hers, and her protests were lost. "Say you love me." Then his mouth brushed her cheek, and he kissed her again.

"He won't let me go. I asked Niall—"

Alex covered her lips with his fingertips. "Don't say it. I won't hear his name." When he slipped his fingers away, his mouth covered hers. "Tell me," he whispered into her hair as he held her against him. "Say you feel the same."

"Yes," she whispered.

He held her soft face moistened with tears. "I love you. How could you not have known it?"

He combed his fingers into her hair, slipped off the ribbon that held it, and inhaled the scent of her hair. As he released it, he traced a line with his finger from her ear to the edge of her collar. "It's like silk."

Kenna lifted her chin and took a halting breath. "It's too late for us."

"Shh." He touched her lips then kissed her again.

She pulled away. His excitement of being with her gave way to grief over what they had lost.

"How many times will you break my heart?"

He looked at her. "You cannae marry him."

"Then why did you tell me to do it?" Her voice was quiet and measured.

"I didn't think I would ever feel normal again. When I came home, I couldnae enjoy life. It may as well have been over. When I realized that I loved you, I was sure I would ruin your life."

"And so you have."

Alex lifted his chin and clenched his jaw. She was right. It was done. He could not take it back.

"I will always love you." She buried her face in his chest while he held her. Kenna took a sharp breath. "But now I must go before someone sees us."

He nodded and kissed her. She turned to leave, but he held her hand and pulled her back into his arms. He put his mouth on hers and kissed her as though she were his.

"Let me go," she said breathlessly.

With a groan, he stepped backward. "We will be together."

She shook her head hopelessly.

Alex helped her onto her horse. As she adjusted her foot in the stirrup, Alex touched Kenna's ankle. His fingers spread to grasp her calf. He was forced to let go as she urged her horse forward and rode off toward Callum's house.

Chapter 13

Matter of Trust

ALEX RETURNED WELL AFTER KENNA AND STABLED HIS horse. He went inside and upstairs before anyone noticed him, but he could not resist pausing outside Kenna's door.

As he did so, a voice sounded through the door. "Right away, mistress."

Alex bolted across the hallway and looked casually back while he put his key in the lock. A maid emerged from Kenna's room as Alex opened his door. He stepped inside and waited until she had gone, then he crossed the hallway to Kenna's room and knocked lightly. When she called for the maid to enter, he glanced down the hall in both directions and slipped into her room. Closing the door, he grinned at her surprise.

"Alex! You can't be in here!"

Longing burned in him. "But I am." In three strides, he crossed the room. Only after he had thoroughly kissed her did he release her. "You may breathe now but make haste, for I've a mind to taste your lips again."

"How can you be so full of cheer when so much is wrong?"

His mouth spread in a grin that Kenna found hard to resist. "Because I'm in love." Only when their eyes met did his grin fade. "And we will be together."

"Alex, I wish it could be, but—"

He kissed her to keep her from voicing her doubts. It worked, for Kenna clung to his muscular arms and surrendered.

"Mistress—" came a voice from outside.

Kenna flinched and called to the maid to stop her.

The latch rattled, then the door opened. "I forgot —" The maid stopped in her tracks. "Oh, I-I thought you told me to enter."

No one moved for a moment. Kenna stared. Alex stood a few steps away from the spot he had reached while trying to distance himself from Kenna before the door opened.

"I'm sorry, mistress." The young woman's eyes darted from Kenna, whose hair hung disheveled, to Alex. "I thought—I'm sorry." With a quick curtsy, she turned and scurried away.

Alex closed the door while Kenna tried, with trembling fingers, to put her hair back in place. When that proved impossible, she dropped her arms in frustration and went to the window. Through the clouds, ribbons of morning light cast an uneven glow on the frost-dusted ground.

Alex rested his hands on her shoulders. "I'll talk to her."

"And what can you say that will not make it worse?"

"Kenna." He tried to coax her back into his arms, but she resisted. He circled his arms about her waist from behind.

TOO WRAPPED up in conflicting emotions to sit calmly at breakfast, Kenna waited until later to go downstairs. She found Alex in the study with Mari. Alex stood as Kenna entered.

Mari went to her. Taking her hands, she said, "Alex told us."

With a quick glance at Alex, Kenna nodded. "I see."

Mari gave her a reassuring smile. "We'll get through this."

Kenna almost believed her.

Callum walked in and closed the door. "I spoke with the chambermaid, but she'd already told her mother, the cook, about it. I left them both with a stern warning of the consequences should the story get out." Callum's eyes betrayed his doubt.

Alex agreed. "We can hope, but I'd best go to Sanderson and speak with him directly."

Callum paced the length of the carpet. "You'll do no such thing, you poor *eejit*. You're so lovesick you dinnae ken what you're saying."

Alex leapt forward, nostrils flaring. "Well, I'll not sit here while you pace and ponder."

Callum shot him an accusing look that required no further words.

Alex's hardened expression made clear that he was holding back. He turned instead to practical talk. "We must first stop the wedding."

Kenna said, "'Tis not right to break his heart just to satisfy mine."

Alex scoffed. "Break his heart? He doesnae love you."

"And yet he's marrying her." Callum narrowed his eyes at Alex.

"Not if I can help it," said Alex.

Callum said, "I know Sanderson, as do you. He's a stubborn bastard in matters of business. Dinnae expect him just to walk away. Love or not, he's a proud man."

"And yet not man enough to serve his clan and his king."

Kenna said, "To be fair, he's a widower with five children to care for."

Alex conceded, rolling his eyes. "Oh, aye—the five children. That alone would be enough for a man to seek marriage. Good God, Kenna, did you not think about that?"

She said softly, "I want children."

Caught off guard, Alex stopped in his tracks and looked at her. The thought of her having his children was something he had not considered. It was a feeling quite unlike any he had known.

Still pacing, Callum turned toward the others. "He's a man with ambition. That much is certain."

Pulled from thoughts of Kenna and the family he longed to have with her, Alex said, "While I was away arranging the trust, I started to think about Kenna's life after the wedding."

Callum said, "Best not think about that."

Ignoring him, Alex said, "I thought of how good it would be for Kenna to have her childhood home so close, to visit whenever she wanted some time to herself."

"And with your farm just beyond that—how convenient," said Callum with a hint of a smirk.

Alex said, "I've had enough of your remarks."

"But 'tis what you were thinking, was it not?"

After a pointed look at Callum, Alex went on. "What I was thinking was how convenient her farm was for him. Even without Kenna's land, he would double his livestock. That was when I was certain he was not marrying out of love."

Callum settled back into his chair. "'Tis an interesting theory."

Alex continued. "The fact that a lovely lass came with it to mother his five children—well, that was too much to resist."

Callum's brows rose. "Aye, it could be. He would not be the first to marry for practical reasons. And really, what's wrong with that?"

Alex's eyes narrowed. "What is wrong is that Kenna deserves more."

"She deserves you?" A small spark lit Callum's eyes.

"Aye, she deserves to be loved, not married for the land she owns—or that he thinks she owns." Alex lowered his voice. "My point is, I was not about to give her land so Sanderson could take it from her, which was why I had the solicitor draw up a trust. Now he'll never take her home from her."

"So what do you propose to do now?"

Alex said with bright eyes, "I expect he'll stew over it for a bit, then he will break the betrothal."

"Or he will sue Kenna."

Alex scoffed. "Sue her? For what?"

"For breach of the marriage contract."

"What's to be gained from that? He cannae take her land."

"No, but he could ask for the value of it," Callum said.

"Based on what?"

"His lost expectations."

Alex shook his head. "But the land's in a trust."

"When was the trust created?"

Alex closed his eyes and exhaled then met Callum's knowing look.

Callum said, "The betrothal contract was signed well before your trust."

"But she didnae own the land then."

Callum nodded. "Aye, but Sanderson could argue that she misrepresented her ownership of the land."

Alex flinched. "She would never do that!"

"But I did."

Both men turned toward Kenna.

"I thought it was mine, so when he asked me, I told him it was."

Alex shared a sharp look with Callum then turned to Kenna and said, "It's all right, lass."

Callum exchanged looks with Mari, who was seated by Kenna and trying to console her. Looking at

Kenna, he said, "What we need to ken first is what you want. Alex has not been shy about his feelings and plans, but we've not heard from you. Do you wish to be released from your promise of marriage?"

"Yes," she said without hesitation.

Seeing her reaction, Callum's eyes warmed. "Then we must see what we can do about that."

She lifted her face, full of hope. "Do you think there's really hope?"

Just as Callum started to answer, the door burst open. Sanderson stormed in, followed closely by a frantic housemaid.

"I'm sorry, Mr. MacDonell," the housemaid said, distraught.

Callum dismissed her with a nod and instructions to close the door.

Sanderson looked only at Kenna. "I'll take you home now."

Kenna was stunned, as the others must have been. No one said a word.

Alex stood as Sanderson approached, but Sanderson ignored him. "Come, Mistress McCowan."

Before Kenna could respond, Alex stepped in his way. "May I have a word?"

"You've had all the words I care to hear. Mistress McCowan and I will be married in a week, after which time any words you have to offer shall be spoken to me, and me alone. Mistress McCowan?" Niall's stern face left no doubt that it was a command. He held his outstretched palm closer to Kenna.

Callum shared a quick look with Mari then

stepped closer to Niall and Alex, eyeing both men with caution. "Ladies, would you excuse us please?"

Mari rose to leave with Kenna but stopped when Sanderson said, "She will not leave this room except on my arm."

Mari's gentle smile lit her face. "Mr. Sanderson, if you'll let me borrow Mistress McCowan, I'm sure this can all be resolved." She held her smile with a grace his cold glare did not earn.

Kenna stood her ground. "As it's my fate being discussed, I'll stay here, if you don't mind."

Mari offered a gracious smile to the men across the room then turned to Kenna. In quiet tones the men wouldn't hear, she said, "You're not helping. He'll cling to his pride while you're here. In your absence, the men might stand a chance of forcing him into a corner."

"Mistress MacDonell, you have been very kind to my betrothed, but the time has come for her to return to her home to prepare for our wedding. I'm sure she has much to do. Do you not, Mistress McCowan?" While his words were polite, Sanderson's demeanor was anything but.

Kenna said, "Aye, but in truth, everything is here. Mistress MacDonell has been helping me."

Mari said, "We'll be just down the hall if you need us."

Alex gave Kenna a bolstering look then turned to Sanderson.

Before Alex could speak, Callum smiled and said, "It appears that the ladies have something to attend to that will afford us a few minutes to talk." He nodded to Mari.

"We willnae be long." With generous grace, Mari smiled kindly at Sanderson then hooked her arm in Kenna's and whisked her from the room.

ALEX OPENED HIS MOUTH, but Callum interrupted. "Mr. Sanderson, won't you sit down?"

Sanderson glowered but accepted Callum's invitation.

Callum said, "I will get to the point. Although there was never any intent to mislead, clearly there has been a misunderstanding regarding the McCowan farm."

"I should say so." Sanderson leaned back and rested his hands on the arms of the chair.

"I've discussed it with Mistress McCowan, and she regrets it but understands how you might have made certain assumptions regarding the land."

"I do not hold her to blame."

Callum gave him a courteous nod. "Under the circumstances, Mistress McCowan has asked me to convey her willingness to release you from your promise to marry."

Sanderson bristled and stole a dark look in Alex's direction.

Callum said firmly, "Mistress McCowan expressed this directly to me."

"Did she? Well, it willnae be necessary. The wedding will proceed as planned."

Callum said, "Before you decide, there is more. As you know, while Mistress McCowan has been given the land, it will be held for her in trust. As her future husband, your signature is needed to state that you consent to the trust."

Sanderson leaned back and eyed Callum. "Consent?"

"To the trust," Callum said.

A long silence followed while Sanderson pondered the situation. His eyes lit with a smile. "You need my signature?"

"As a legal formality." Callum placed the contract before him and dipped a pen in the inkwell.

Sanderson took no time to consider the offer. "No, I'll not sign your legal formality."

A long silence hung in the air.

When Sanderson shifted in the chair, Callum said, "I see." He nodded and waited until Sanderson grew uncomfortable enough to adjust his position in the chair again. Callum set the pen down and leaned back. "I'm afraid Mistress McCowan will not marry without it."

Sanderson looked like an animal pacing a cage when he got up and walked to the window. He stared out at the hillside.

Alex could nearly taste his triumph as he and Callum exchanged looks.

Sanderson turned back and returned to his seat. "Very well then. I'll sign it." He reached for the vellum document.

Before he could sign it, Alex stood, nearly knocking over the chair. "Do you not understand what you're doing?" Callum shot Alex a look that would have stopped a lesser man in his tracks, but Alex was unfazed. "She brings nothing to the marriage!"

Sanderson lifted his chin at Alex. "Except for herself, which is all I desire." He glanced away but turned back to Alex. "Oh, and of course her movable property, which includes several dozen head of cattle."

Alex pounded his fist on the desk. "Take the cattle. Just let her go."

"Why? Because you want me to?" He looked at Alex, who was fuming.

"Because she doesnae love you!"

Sanderson seemed calmer. "You've been an arrogant arse since we were bairns. I've watched you break that girl's heart for years, but you were too caught up in yourself to see it. But I saw. She deserves someone better than you."

"Someone whom she doesnae love?"

Sanderson said dispassionately, "No one forced her to say yes. But now that she's promised to me, you've decided you want her." He lifted his chin. "Well, you cannae have her."

Alex lunged for him, but Callum leapt forward and held him back. Alex said, "You hedgeborn bastard."

Sanderson practically smiled as he turned to Callum. "Please convey my regrets to Mistress McCowan for leaving without saying good-bye. She clearly is busy. I am too, so I must take my leave. Keep her here, if you like. The brief separation will make our wedding night sweeter."

Alex lurched, but Callum tightened his grip and muttered a warning that stopped him.

"I would shake your hand, Callum, but I see that your hands are full at the moment." With a satisfied grin, Sanderson strode to the door.

After he had gone, Mari and Kenna came into the study. Mari stopped when she saw Callum's grip Alex's arm.

Still burning with rage, Alex gave a dismissive nod and sank into a chair, where he buried his face in his hands. Kenna's blanched face was her only outward sign of emotion as she went to Alex and put her hand on his shoulder. He held it tightly.

When he had sufficiently swallowed his anger, he looked up and said, "I will not let him have you."

Mari went to Callum. "I gather it did not go well."

Callum gave her a look that required no further discussion.

Alex said, "I dinnae ken why, but the man despises me—so much so that, from sheer spite, he'll not let you go."

Kenna said, "What can we do?"

Alex glanced at the unsigned document on the table. "He has not signed the trust. God's teeth, that's my fault, as well." He thought back on the moment when Sanderson might have signed it, but Alex's angry outburst had interrupted him. He looked at Callum, who had the good grace not to mention what they both were recalling. Alex went on. "Well, no matter. It served its purpose and failed. The trust did not deter him."

"He could take my home from me?"

Callum said, "Not unless you go through with the

wedding. If you were to wed without his agreeing to the trust, it would not be valid."

Kenna said, "But if he won't agree, then what choice have I?"

Callum said, "I wouldnae underestimate him. His hatred for Alex confounds the mind."

"Then what's to be done?"

Alex grasped her hands. His ardent gaze locked onto hers. "You must break your promise."

"I've already asked him to release me, and he refused."

"This time, dinnae give him a choice."

Kenna walked to the window and looked at the land she had roamed upon freely when they were all children. A long while passed before she said, "Very well. I'll tell him today."

"No. Tell him nothing," Alex said.

Confusion creased her brow as she faced him. "But if I dinnae break our betrothal, then what can I do?"

"Run away," Alex said without hesitation. "Aye, we'll run away and get married before he can stop us." Alex lifted her hands to his lips. "If you will have me."

Callum said, "Would you take her from the home you've worked so hard to give her?"

"No. We'll return."

"Man, think of the scandal," said Callum.

"In time people will forget."

"Perhaps, but that time can be long."

Mari said, "Some will forgive, and the rest will grow tired of talking about it."

Alex said, "I dinnae care about what they say."

Saddened, Mari said, "But what of Kenna—and your children?"

A gentle smile formed on Kenna's lips. "Our children will know love. They will understand because we will teach them what love is and why it's worth fighting for—even if others dinnae understand."

Alex squeezed Kenna's hand.

Callum shook his head. "If you break the betrothal, I have no doubt he'll take you to court for breach of promise."

"But what would he gain? Surely he cannae force me to marry him if I'm already married."

"No," Callum said. "But the court could grant him a remedy. He could ask for the land."

"And the cattle," said Alex. "For it would have been his after the wedding."

"Give it to him," said Kenna.

"I offered it to him. Forgive me. I ken it wasnae mine to give."

Callum said, "It'll take money to fight a breach of promise suit in court."

Kenna shook her head. "I've not been able to keep up the farm as it was when my father and brother were here. I've barely enough to keep it going."

Alex sank into a chair. "When we left, I sold all my cattle. I've some money saved, but not enough for this sort of fight. Sanderson will not give up easily."

Mari said, "We've put all that we have into building our home."

"There's precious little left, but we'll do what we're able," said Callum.

Kenna's face brightened. "I'm not married yet, so the cattle are still mine, are they not?"

With a hopeless shrug, Alex said, "For now, but Sanderson will ask for the livestock as movable property that you would have brought into the marriage."

"But what if I sold it?"

Alex lifted his chin. "Sold it?"

Callum said, "It is hers. I suppose she's got the right to sell it."

"Aye, she could." Smiling, Alex glanced at Callum, whose eyes glimmered. "It would be enough to pay for a solicitor, with some left over, perhaps." He pulled Kenna into his arms.

"To begin a new life together," said Kenna.

"No, I'll not take what's yours," Alex said firmly.

Kenna looked at him with a sly smile. "We can discuss that after the sale. Right now, I'd like to know who will buy my cattle?"

Callum folded his arms, deep in thought. "No one here, but perhaps in Fort William."

"Fort William?" Alex nodded with brightening eyes. "Aye."

Chapter 14

The Reivers

THE FOUR *REIVERS* STOPPED AT THE CREST OF THE HILL and looked down at the grazing cattle.

Callum turned to Alex and smiled. "Shall we?"

Alex nodded, and the two men took off down the hill with Kenna and Mari close behind. The dim glow of the predawn sun lit their way as they drove Mari's herd to the drover's road that led to Fort William. Skilled drovers might have made the trip in two days, but they didn't want word of their plan to get back to Sanderson, so they set off alone. With four dozen cattle, they hoped to make it to Fort William in three days.

While Kenna had helped out on cattle drives, it was all new to Mari. But they managed to keep the cows moving along the trail. They didn't relax until the late afternoon when they felt sure they had avoided Sanderson's notice. They stopped in a meadow with a small stream running through it. With winter's cold upon them, Callum started a fire, and they warmed themselves. Too tired for talk, they all soon fell asleep, with the men taking turns keeping watch.

In the morning, they huddled close to the fire and ate bannocks.

"What if we cannae find a buyer?" asked Kenna.

Alex said, "If we cannae find anyone else, I know one interested buyer."

Surprised, she asked, "Who?"

Alex grinned broadly. "I had a sudden desire to buy cattle. Isn't that so, Callum?"

"Aye, he did. He was just telling me so." Callum's eyes betrayed the grin that was forming.

Mari looked at Kenna and shrugged.

"But you said—"

"I ken what I said, but I've enough to keep the cattle until spring, when there should be more buyers."

"But why go through all this when I could just keep them?"

Alex put his arm about her and drew her closer. "We want to remove any reason for Sanderson to fight for you. I'm hoping that, without your cattle, you'll be less attractive to Sanderson."

"And what about you?"

"Me?"

Kenna tilted her head and looked at him sideways. "Will you still find me attractive without my cattle?"

Alex frowned with a glint in his eye. "Well, that could be a problem." He leaned closer and spoke in seductive tones. "Some men fancy a pretty face or long auburn tresses." He combed a hand into the hair at the nape of her neck and leaned closer until his lips nearly touched hers. "Or soft lips that want kissing." He brushed his lips against hers until her breath halted. Then Alex leaned back and said with gusto, "But I do like a woman with cows."

"*Och*!" Kenna swatted him, but he caught her wrist.

Still laughing, he pulled her into his arms. "Of course, I cannae pay much. I'm afraid all I can afford to pay is one kiss per head of cattle, so I'd best begin paying."

He was taking his time with the first payment when Callum cleared his throat loudly. "As your chaperone, it's my duty to tell you to douse that fire. While you're at it, you can douse the campfire too."

Alex grumbled and gave Kenna a kiss on the forehead, then he set about packing for the day's journey. As clan chief, Callum's father had friends in Fort William who, as a favor to him, would—if not buy them—look after the cattle until they were sold. That would free them all up for a hasty return to settle their business with Sanderson before the wedding was scheduled to take place.

On the second day, they covered more ground, and their quickened pace lifted everyone's spirits. The sun was close to the horizon when they found grazing land with water and stopped for the night. The warmth of the fire, combined with their fatigue, brought sleep quickly for all except Kenna. It was her turn to keep watch. In the night, an agitated moaning drew Kenna's attention. The moon cast a faint light on Alex, who was tossing his head from side to side.

She knelt beside him. "Alex?" When his groaning continued, Kenna gripped his shoulders and gently shook him, but his moaning grew frantic. "Alex, you're having a dream." Kenna tried to speak softly so as not to awaken the others, but he wasn't responding.

Alex cried out and spun her around, pinning her face to the ground while he pressed both her wrists to her back.

"Alex." When she opened her mouth to cry out his name, dirt stuck to her lips. "Alex!"

The pressure disappeared. Kenna sat up, coughing and wiping dirt from her mouth, to find Callum holding Alex. Alex looked back at Callum with unfocused eyes.

"He has nightmares," said Kenna.

Callum peered at her. "And how would you know?"

"Never mind. I found out by chance." She went toward Alex, but Callum held out his arm to stop her. "Alex?"

His face fraught with concern, Alex tore his attention from Kenna and looked at Callum, who still had a firm grip on his shoulders. "What's happened?"

Callum said, "You were hurting the lass."

"You were having a dream," Kenna said as Mari put comforting hands on Kenna's shoulders.

Alex cursed and shook himself free. "Are you hurt?"

"No, I'm fine. I'm just worried about you."

"I'm sorry, hen. It was a dream." With a quick look at Callum and Mari, he apologized then went to Kenna and lifted her hands. "Try to go back to sleep." He kissed her hand and sent her to lie down.

THE REST of their journey went smoothly but slowly. Alex said little about his nightmare, except that he still had them but less frequently.

They awoke on the fourth day to a dusting of snow and thick mist. With their spirits already low, the weather did not sit well with them.

Alex stared into the haze. "We'll have to wait until it clears."

"We haven't got time," Kenna said. "It's three days until the wedding."

Callum said, "I'll not drive the cattle over a cliff."

He was right, but the whole situation made her uneasy. After all, the wedding day loomed closer, and she had no real hope of release.

Alex took Kenna's hand and led her on a short walk. When they were out of earshot of Callum and Mari, Alex stopped and looked into her eyes. "Hen, what's bothering you?"

Kenna shook her head. "I know Callum's right to wait, but I just want to get there and be done with it all. I want everything out in the open so we can look forward to being together." She lifted her eyes to meet his, and his tender gaze reassured her.

He held her shoulders. "I love you, and I'll be with you until you beg me to leave you alone." His lips spread in a smile. "Now, quick, give us a hug before your gatekeeper sees we're alone."

Kenna sank into the warm strength of his chest, and he held her and stroked her hair. He lifted her chin and kissed her. No more worries could plague her while she was in Alex's arms.

Callum's voice startled them both. "If you two

have no objection, I thought we might be on our way to Fort William."

Kenna turned, beaming, toward Callum, who gave Alex a look with an uplifted eyebrow.

Alex put his hand on the small of Kenna's back and urged her along. "You heard the man. We've no time to tarry."

By midday, they could see the road ahead far enough to proceed slowly. Alex cast Kenna reassuring looks. By late afternoon, they were losing the light.

Callum said, "I know where we are. There's a field just over this hill."

Within the hour, they'd arrived and were welcomed by Aodhan MacDuff and his wife, Gilda. They offered the reivers a hot meal and lodging for the night. They dined well, for MacDuff was a prosperous farmer with a good eye for business that had afforded him a most comfortable home. In the warm glow of the fireplace and wall sconces, they ate heaping plates of Scotch collops, mashed potatoes, and toast. With it, they drank some of MacDuff's finest whisky and left all memories of the cold cattle drive behind them.

From there, it was a short ride to Fort William in the morning. A light rain fell as they rode into town.

Kenna looked at Alex, who couldn't seem to stop smiling. "You seem in awfully good spirits on this gloomy day."

"Gloomy day? That's no way to refer to your wedding day, lass."

"My what?"

Alex grinned and offered his arm. "Come with me,

Mistress McCowan. Rain or not, I've a mind to be married today."

Kenna stopped and stared at him. "Have you? And you didnae think to mention it to me?"

He appeared stunned and a little crestfallen. "You've not changed your mind, have you?"

"No!" Kenna laughed. "But I wish I'd known."

"I wanted to surprise you."

The disappointment on his face made Kenna almost regret having said anything. "Well, you have. I love the idea of it but—well, look at me!" She looked down at the clothes she had worn droving cattle for four days. "I've nothing to wear, and I smell like a cow!"

"Aye, but a bonny one!" Alex winked, which further frustrated Kenna. He hastened to add, "Come with me. I think we can remedy this." His eyes lost their spark as he searched her face. "That is, if you would have me as your husband."

"Aye, my *braw* man, I would. But I thought we'd decided not to run away."

Alex seemed almost embarrassed, the corner of his mouth turning up just a bit. "Aye, but as he'll most likely sue either way, I saw no reason to wait. The truth is, I cannae wait any longer, for I love you so much."

"People will talk."

"We'll not listen to them." Alex gazed into her eyes. "Will you marry me, Kenna?"

"Aye."

"Today?"

Kenna's eyes brightened as the thought took hold in her mind. "Aye."

"Are you certain?"

Kenna grinned. "You had best stop asking. My answer might change."

Alex laughed. "Very well then, mistress. Come with me."

Kenna took his arm, and he led her to an inn, where Callum met them and showed them to their rooms. Inside Kenna's room, Mari waited.

"I'll go tell them to bring up the hot water," Mari said and left.

Kenna gasped with delight. Not only would she have a luxurious bath but laid out on the bed was a simple, clean yellow jacket, stays, two petticoats, an apron, stockings, and shoes. An hour later, Kenna was clean, dressed, and neatly coiffed. Mari opened the door, and there Alex stood.

Kenna's heart leapt at the sight of him dressed in a smart doublet and plaid. He was clean-shaven with his sand-colored hair touching his collar. There stood the man she had loved nearly all of her life, holding out his hand for her. She barely noticed Callum and Mari as they followed them.

On the way, Alex explained that theirs could not be a church wedding. "Crying the banns would have too great a risk of word reaching home. Do you mind very much?"

"How could I? I'm with you, and soon we'll be married." Kenna felt a proper fool, for she couldn't stop smiling.

Alex shrugged. "Then we will marry today, and no one will part us."

It had rained through the morning, but as they

walked to the blacksmith, the rain lightened to a drizzle. Callum had arranged for the blacksmith to be ready upon their arrival. Alex and Kenna took their places with Callum and Mari beside them. Alex took her hands. Mari looked at Callum and smiled. The blacksmith was beginning to speak when footsteps approached.

"Aren't you forgetting the groom?"

Alex and Kenna turned to find Sanderson, arms folded, before them.

Chapter 15

In the Firelight

"Leave us, for you've no business here." Alex stepped toward Sanderson, but Callum grabbed his arm. "I'll not stand by while this whoreson ruins my wedding."

"I've more right to say that than you," Sanderson said with the confidence of a man who had nothing more to lose.

Alex said, "The difference is that she loves me."

"But she's promised to me."

"Only because in a weak moment, you took advantage of her."

"You're talking nonsense," Sanderson said.

"Am I? Soon after, she told you she'd made a mistake, and she asked you to release her."

"She made a promise, and I relied on it."

"But she doesnae love you."

Kenna stepped forward. "I'll speak for myself." She lifted her chin. "Mr. Sanderson, I'm sorry, but I cannae marry you."

"Kenna." Alex started toward her.

She held out a firm hand. "No, 'tis my turn to speak. You both act like I've no mind of my own. Well, I do. Alex, we wouldnae be here but for you." She cast him a chastising look.

He clenched his jaw and said nothing.

Sanderson snickered, drawing Kenna's attention back to him.

"I'm sorry, Niall. Truly, I am." She took a sharp breath. His bitter expression chilled her to the marrow, but she continued. "I've been unfair to you, and I deeply regret it. Forgive me, but it would not be right to marry you when I love someone else. Please dinnae ask it of me. We were friends once. Let us not lose that."

While her words appeared to mollify him, they had also cut into a wound that was already open, and his eyes burned with pain. "You cannae marry him. He'll only hurt you again."

"That is my choice to make," Kenna said softly.

"You lost that choice when you promised yourself to me. Now step aside. I dinnae want you to get hurt." He stepped forward, but Kenna held up her palm, and he stopped.

She spoke gently. "Go home, Niall, for I'll not marry you."

Alex stood by her side, his hand on her shoulder. "I'm sorry for the pain we have caused you, but you must let her go."

Sanderson's eyes darted to the blacksmith, who stood ready to proceed with a fight or a wedding—

whichever came next. Sanderson's gaze settled on Kenna, and she met his bitter gaze.

"I'm sorry, Niall."

Sanderson's pain hardened to bitterness. "'Tis wrong what you've both done, and I'll see that you pay. A curse on all who take part in this wedding." He stormed off, leaving them stunned.

Mari put her hand on Kenna's shoulder.

"He'll never let me be happy," Kenna said.

"In time, he'll realize that he would not have been happy if you didnae love him."

"He cursed us—and you too."

While Mari consoled Kenna, Callum pulled Alex aside. "I dinnae trust him. There's a bit of madness in his eyes. We'd best be on our guard. I could send a messenger to Aodhan MacDuff to ask for some men."

"I see no need for that," Alex said. "Sanderson is alone, and no match for either of us—let alone both together."

"Aye, but it's your wedding day, and your mind is elsewhere."

Alex couldn't help but smile. "Aye, it is that. Sanderson cannae ruin that for us. We'll not let him." With renewed spirit, he went to Kenna. "'Tis our day, lass. Come marry me now."

Kenna looked at Alex's broad smile and smiled back. "Are you sure?"

Alex laughed. "Sure? After all we've gone through?" He swept her into his arms and swung her around. He set her down, kissed her, and led her back to the blacksmith. "We've come for a wedding, so marry us now." His voice had a confident spark that he hoped would put Kenna at ease.

"I cannae do it," said the blacksmith, fear in his eyes.

"What?" Callum stepped forward.

The blacksmith, a burly man who towered above them all, shook his head. "I'll not bring on a curse just for marrying you."

"A curse?" Alex couldn't find words for a moment. "Are you talking about what that clod Sanderson said?"

"I'll not meddle with curses." The blacksmith walked away.

"Are we cursed already?" Kenna asked.

"*Och*, hen, come here." Alex held Kenna while he shared a dark look with Callum and Mari.

"Come, lass," said Callum. "He's not the only blacksmith in Scotland. We'll ride to the next town and find someone tomorrow."

"Aye," Alex said with false cheer.

"Let's all go to yon tavern and forget about this," Callum said.

He put his hand firmly on Alex's shoulder, and they all walked away from the blacksmith's shop, leaving all that had happened behind them. At the tavern, they supped and let the ale take the sting from their troubles. When their thoughts returned to Sanderson, they switched from ale to whisky. By evening, Callum had poured enough whisky for Alex and Kenna to feel free from worry, as well as their senses.

Callum caught Mari's disapproving eye and shrugged. "Well, he's feeling less pain."

While Alex was well-practiced in holding his whisky, Kenna was not. She was draped over Alex's chest and shoulders, and his hands roamed freely through her hair and across her shoulders. Her skin was so soft that he could not resist stroking her neck with his fingertips.

As his hands strayed down her throat and slipped just inside the edge of her neckline, Callum gave him a jab in the ribs. "We're not in a brothel, you rake, and you're not married yet. Show the lass some respect."

"Sorry, hen." Alex lifted Kenna's chin, only to find she had fallen asleep. He lay her head back on his shoulder and looked at Callum, who was laughing. "Oh, aye, you're happy now, aren't you."

Mari smiled sympathetically.

Alex gazed at his sleeping would-be bride. "Let's get you to bed, lass." He raised an eyebrow at Callum. "To sleep. Alone. As will I."

THE FOLLOWING MORNING, they left for home. While Alex awoke feeling renewed, Kenna had not fared so well. She didn't complain, but she didn't smile either. A quiet moan came from her every now and then. By midday, the gray mist had become a full downpour, so they stopped in the small village of Achnacarry. It had an inn and a blacksmith, so Callum secured two rooms for the night, and the four of them went to the blacksmith. Under an oilcloth awning, with rain pouring down around them, the blacksmith commenced with the wedding.

Alex put a ring that had belonged to his mother on Kenna's finger and plighted his troth. All else seemed to fade to a blur of sights and sounds as he looked into her eyes. And then it was over, and they were married. He took her face in his hands, and he kissed her.

Kenna looked into Alex's eyes. "Is it true?" She turned to the blacksmith. "Are we married now?"

He let out a hearty laugh. "Aye."

Alex kissed her and held her against him, then he fixed his eyes on her in wonder. "I didnae think I could love anyone so."

Callum and Mari exchanged fond looks.

Mari said, "We must celebrate! Let's get out of this rain and go sit by a fire."

There was a pub downstairs in the inn where they were staying, and thanks to the early hour, there were still seats by the fireplace. Callum and Mari spoke to the owner, who stood behind the bar while, without a word, Alex led Kenna upstairs to their room. Once inside, he closed the door. Kenna gasped from the sudden force of his arms pulling her against him, and he pressed his mouth to hers with a devouring kiss. When he released her, he held her face and looked at her with that same feeling of wonder he had felt after the wedding.

Kenna's lips parted, and her chest swelled. "You take my breath away."

"Wife." He mulled over the sound of that. "Wife, I've a mind not to go back downstairs." His eyes had a mischievous light. When Kenna said nothing, he kissed her again. "You'd best put up a fight, for my good sense escapes me."

Kenna stood on her toes, put her arms about his neck, and kissed him. She touched his face then let her fingers slide down his neck to his shoulders.

Alex gripped her wrists and put distance between them. "God's teeth, you tempt me. But if we dinnae return to them soon, I'll not hear the end of it."

Kenna whispered, "I've wanted to kiss you all day, and every day before that."

Alex's brow creased as he lifted her chin and looked into her eyes. "I'll kiss you each day for as long as you'll have me." With a tender kiss, he took her hand and led her downstairs.

Callum had told the barkeep of the wedding, so when they came downstairs, a cheer rang out in the room. Kenna blushed, and Alex laughed and gave Callum a well-deserved glare. Callum grinned and handed them each a drink. There were toasts, and a fiddle played. Someone joined in with a drum, and a few others sang. There was dancing and laughter. In that room full of strangers, their joy was complete. They were married and would be together.

Sometime later, Alex gripped Callum's shoulder and said something. Callum patted his back and turned to Kenna. He and Mari each bade her good-night, and Alex and Kenna went up the stairs to the sound of ribald cheers.

Back inside their room, Alex closed and bolted the door. A fire bathed the room in warm light. Mari had left candles about, and Kenna lit them. Alex took the candle she held and blew it out. He stepped closer until their bodies were touching. Kenna put her arms about his neck, but he gently lowered them. His gaze held hers as he touched her neck and his fingertips felt their way along her collar. Desire burned in his eyes, but he took his time unfastening her woolen waistcoat and sliding it off her shoulders. Next he unlaced the stays and unfastened her petticoats, then she stood before him in only her shift and stockings.

Kenna took in a sharp breath as he took her face in his hands and kissed her until she had to steady herself by gripping the cloth of his leine. With a hoarse whisper, he uttered her name. His palms slid down her breasts, her waist, and her hips until he was on his knees. He reached up under her shift and pulled down one stocking, then the other. One hand worked up her legs until his touch made her breathing grow shallow. She doubted whether she could remain standing for long.

In one instant, he rose, hoisted her into his arms, and took her to the bed. He hastily unwrapped his plaid and nearly tore off his leine and boots. Kenna lay on the bed, watching until he stood *braw* and bare before her.

"What?" he asked as though she had spoken.

"I said nothing."

"But you're thinking something, and I wish to know it."

"Nothing." She felt shy, which wasn't like her.

He lay beside her, his lips inches from hers. "What is it?"

"I was admiring you."

Alex smiled. "I was thinking the same about you."

He kissed her. "And how I plan to admire every part of your body before the night's over."

He spoke little more as he took his time making good on his promise. When he entered her carefully, she winced from the pain.

"It will not always hurt," he assured her.

He touched her until she forgot about pain and felt only the thrill and the fullness of him. He clutched at the linens with his need to be farther inside her. She wanted him closer until they were one and lay spent in the flickering light from the fire.

Chapter 16

The Journey Home

CALLUM WATCHED ALEX DIG INTO HIS SECOND HELPING of smoked beef, cheese, fresh eggs, and thick slices of bread slathered with butter and currant jelly.

"Hungry, are you?" The corner of Callum's mouth twitched.

Without bothering to glance up, Alex nodded and kept eating.

Kenna narrowed her eyes at Callum then turned to Mari, who diverted her eyes to her food. Kenna exhaled with a hint of impatience. "That man's always hungry, in case you haven't noticed."

Alex set down his ale and gave Kenna a warm smile. "Now that I've had a fine and satisfying meal, I'm no longer hungry—for the moment." He looked Callum in the eye long enough to punctuate the point, then he leaned back and put his arm about Kenna's shoulders.

"Good," Callum said with a glint in his eyes.

"Then you're ready to climb back into the saddle and spend the day riding."

Mari turned away as if she had not heard him. Alex tilted his head and gave Callum a withering look.

Seeing the exchange, Kenna said, "God's teeth! Do you not think I ken what you're talking about? Well, I do. No one's laughing!"

And no one was, nor were they speaking. Alex stared at Kenna while Callum leaned back, stunned. Then Mari laughed. That set the others off laughing as well. Callum called for a round of whisky to warm them before their journey. Not long after, they were on their way home.

A COLD HIGHLAND wind blew across the road as they reached the outskirts of the village and came upon a woman walking alone. As they rode past, she looked up and caught Alex's eye.

"Mr. MacDonnell?" she said.

Both Alex and Callum turned, but it was Alex who answered her. "Rose, is that you?" He dismounted and went to her while Callum exchanged looks with Mari. "What happened? Where are you going?"

Rose's eyes filled with tears. "When I got home, the man who was going to marry me said I was damaged. After all, I'd run away, so there's only one thing that could have happened to me. He refused to marry me. He wasnae very nice about it either."

"I'm sorry," said Alex.

Kenna dismounted and joined them.

Alex said, "Rose, I'd like you to meet my wife, Kenna MacDonell."

She offered Kenna her hand and shook it vigorously. "'Tis a pleasure to meet you, Mistress MacDonell."

Callum cleared his throat, prompting Alex to introduce Rose to the rest of the party. Standing beside Kenna, he saw she was a few inches shorter. Unlike his wife's delicate face, Rose had strong cheekbones and wide, earnest eyes.

With the introductions accomplished, Alex turned to Kenna. "I met Rose when I came to Fort William to draw up your trust." Seeing that Kenna's pleasant smile didn't entirely mask the doubt in her eyes, he added, "Rose had some troubles, and I helped her with them."

Alex looked into Kenna's eyes and found the same gentle gaze that never failed to retrace the connection between them. The circumstances surrounding the stranger might cause any wife to have questions. Hidden by the folds of her skirts, he gave Kenna's hand a squeeze to drive away any lingering doubt.

Turning to Rose, he said, "Where are you going?"

"My father said no one would have me now, so he told me to go back where I came from. I remembered what you said, so I hoped I might find you in Fort William."

Alex nodded and turned to Kenna. "I told Rose to come find me if anything happened."

"That was kind of you," Callum said with a wry look.

"Aye, well I have my moments," Alex said with a sharp look at Callum.

"He's a very kind man!" Rose smiled, unaware of the barbs the two men were exchanging.

Alex did his best to ignore Callum. "I dinnae ken how our paths failed to cross."

Rose lowered her eyes. "They did. You were celebrating. I dinnae want Mistress—"

"MacDonell," said Alex.

With a worried expression, she finished the thought. "Mistress MacDonell to think the wrong thing."

"But why leave Fort William?"

"They found me asleep on the street and took me to the poor house. It's a terrible place. So I sneaked out and started to walk."

Mari said, "You must be hungry." She pulled Rose aside to sit and offered her some of the food the innkeeper had packed for their journey.

While Rose ate and talked with Mari, Alex pulled Kenna aside. "I ken what you must think."

She said, "I trust you, but I dinnae ken her."

"*Och*, she's like a wee sister."

"Except she's not very wee."

He lifted her chin with his fingertips. "This man loves no other but you."

"I don't doubt it. But I was no older than she when I first fell in love, and love is a powerful thing."

He slipped his arms about her waist and pulled her against him. "Aye, my love. So it is." He glanced over to make sure no one would see, and he stole a kiss.

His soft lips on hers made her knees buckle. She

had no doubt he could have a similar effect upon other women. "Tread carefully, Alex."

"My heart is yours, and it always will be."

Kenna touched his chest. "This heart is precious to me."

Callum cleared his throat loudly. "What would you have us do regarding that lass over there?"

Alex glanced at Kenna, but before he could answer, Kenna said, "We should help her, as we would anyone else in need."

Alex kissed her forehead then turned his attention to Callum. "From the looks of her, she'll not make it far on her own."

Kenna said, "We must bring her with us."

"Are you certain?" Alex looked doubtful.

"I am."

Callum said, "She can stay at our house until arrangements can be made."

"No, she can stay at my house." Kenna turned to Alex. "I'll not be staying there now. She can look after it until she decides what to do."

Surprised, Alex said, "I suppose she could."

Kenna smiled. "Good. She can take my horse, and I'll ride with you—if you dinnae mind."

"Not at all," Alex said with a spark in his eyes.

HOURS LATER, they left Callum and Mari at their home. Then Alex and Kenna saw Rose settled in Kenna's cottage, where she would stay for the time being. A short ride down the lane brought them to

Alex's farm, where they left their horses with the stable lad.

Kenna cried out as Alex scooped her into his arms and heaved her over his shoulder to carry her over the threshold. "That's not how it's done!"

Alex let out a hearty laugh. "I'll do as I please, so you'd best get used to it, woman."

As he set her down, Kenna opened her mouth to complain, but he covered it with a kiss. By the time he was finished, she forgot what she'd wanted to say.

"Dinnae think you'll win every argument that way." She put her fists on her waist and looked sternly at him.

"I dinnae ken we were having an argument." He slipped his arms through the gaps left by her bent elbows and drew her against him. He gave her a deep, soul-searching gaze. "Tell me, hen, what have I done to vex you?"

She lowered her gaze. "Well, vex is a bit strong."

"Displeased, then?" His gaze softened, as did her heart. "Lass, are you displeased with me?"

"Well, no, not exactly." She was no longer sure what she had felt, for what she felt now was all that she cared about anymore.

"What is it, then?" His lips parted as he brushed a strand of hair from her forehead.

While he studied her troublesome hair, she found her gaze fixed on his lips. She was drawn to those lips.

"Kenna?"

"Oh. Well, I just thought you'd carry me differently from how you might carry a sack of grain." She was pleased with herself for even remembering.

"Oh, my love, you're so right." After pausing to consider, he said, "Hmm. Now, how is it properly done exactly?"

"Well, you would lift me, well, like so." She held out both arms, palms extended.

He nodded like a proper pupil. With what appeared to be deep concentration, he turned her so she faced away from him. "So one arm goes here?" He slid one arm slowly down from her waist to her knees, then did it again, just to be sure. "And the other... here?" His arm at the small of her back seemed harmless enough until he brought his body against hers and slipped his hand about her waist.

His warm breath brushed her ear, and she took a breath. She lifted her chin as she sighed. Alex held her chin and turned her until her lips opened to his. He devoured her mouth then lifted her and carried her up the remaining stairs and down the short hallway to his bedroom. Once there, he fumbled to open the door. Kenna helped with the latch, and he swept her inside and kicked the door closed.

After he set her down, he said, "How was that?"

"How was what?"

His mouth curved up at the corner. "The lift? Was it to your liking?"

"Aye, it was fine," she whispered.

"Good." He turned and strode to the door.

"Alex!" She rushed after him. "Alex, wait!"

Without turning, he paused at the door. "Why, hen, is something the matter?" He turned and, seeing her, grinned.

"Why, I hope you've enjoyed yourself—playing with my feelings."

"No, not nearly enough." He put his soft lips on hers. His hands moved along her stays to the knotted laces, which he frantically worked to untie. "On the way home, I unlaced these dozens of times in my mind."

While he busied himself with the laces, Kenna ran her palms over his muscular shoulders and chest.

"God's teeth, these irritate me to no end," he said as he pulled the long laces through the eyelets.

Kenna laughed. "I'll admit, you're much easier to unclothe." She unbuckled his belt, pulled it free, and let it drop to the floor. She worked the plaid through his busy arms until that lay on the floor. All that was left was his leine. Her hands roamed freely over his powerful body.

He gripped her wrist and pushed it away. "I've no need of help there, so you'd best put that hand to use here, with these infernal laces."

As she pulled the lace through the last eyelet, Alex pulled off her stays and hurled it across the room. Kenna laughed, but it was gone with a gasp when Alex cupped her breasts and brushed his lips over her linen shift. He pulled it over her head and clutched it in his fist as he kissed her. He was forced to pull his mouth from hers long enough to pull his leine over his head. With a groan, he pulled her bare body against his. Hard and ready for her, he carried her to the bed, set her down, and pulled off her stockings.

Kenna clutched his shoulders and hair as he sent waves of pleasure through her until her head swam. As she heard her own ecstatic moan, he plunged into her with a need that made her want him even more. With each thrust, she clutched any part of his body she could, just to get him farther inside. He exhaled and lay over her, panting. When his breathing was steady, he tenderly kissed her and rolled over to lie on his back beside her.

Kenna awoke to find herself alone, covered by a quilt. Alex crouched by the fireplace, building a fire. She sat up, holding the quilt about her.

He turned and, seeing her, smiled. "And just what thoughts are making you smile so, Mistress MacDonell?"

Her eyes danced. "I was thinking of you."

He raised his eyebrow and came back to bed. "Oh, were you? Tell me more."

Chapter 17

The Visit

ROSE SET A CUP OF HOT TEA ON THE TABLE AND SAT with a contented sigh. While her future was far from certain, she had food and shelter and good people she hoped might one day become friends. Still, she felt an emptiness that could only be filled by her own home and family. She glanced about the snug cottage and felt content for the first time in months.

A loud knock at the door made her flinch. Rose went to the curtain to peek through a gap. A child sat in a wagon and wailed with no adult in sight. She flung open the door but found herself face-to-face with a stranger—an angry one, at that.

He called, "MacDonell!"

"He's not here." She pulled up to her full height and looked at the tall man with as fierce an expression as she could muster.

He took a step to walk past her, but Rose didn't budge. The man glowered then peered over her head to see that the cottage was empty.

"He's not here?" he asked.

"I said as much, did I not? Now if you'll excuse me, there's a crying child, and someone ought to take care of it."

"*Och*, they're like that all day."

"I'm not surprised, if this is any example of the attention they receive!" She rushed past him and went to the wagon.

She found five young children, the oldest no more than eight. A quick inspection showed her that the crying child, who seemed somewhere in the middle of the others age-wise, had no obvious injuries.

She picked him up and said, "Now there, young sir, what is the matter with you?"

The eldest boy said, "*Och*, he's a wee devil. He tried to climb out of the wagon, so I boxed his ears."

"Did you?" She gave him a disappointed look that sent his eyes downward. Meanwhile, she turned her attention to the child on her hip, who had stopped crying. "What's your name, laddie?"

"Robbie."

"Well, Robbie, who is this lad over here?"

"He's my brother."

"I see. Would you introduce me to him?"

Minutes later, she knew all their names. Their hands either clutched hers or her skirt—whichever was nearest—and she led them inside for some biscuits and milk.

Rose tossed a disapproving glance at the man she assumed was their father. "I suppose you've a name too."

"Niall Sanderson, Mistress—"

"McLeod. Rose McLeod," she said with a nod. "You may come inside too—but I'll have no more shouting."

Before long, the children had finished their treats and were on their way outside to play.

Before she would excuse them, Rose gave them a firm look and said, "Later, I'll have biscuits for children with proper behavior, but cross children will go without."

They all nodded and walked properly to the door before taking off in a full run together. Rose smiled until she looked back and saw Niall Sanderson staring at her.

"So what brings you here, Mistress McLeod? Are you kin to Mistress McCowan?" he asked.

"She's now Mistress MacDonnell."

His expression clouded over. "Aye, so she is."

His eyes grew so dark and distant that Rose felt the need to speak, if only to remind him that she was still there. "We're not kin, but I've come here to stay until I can find work."

"And your family? There are some McLeods just past that mountain. Would they be your folk?"

"No. I'm quite alone, and I'll be needing work. So if you hear of anything, it would be a great help if you told me."

Mr. Sanderson nodded and once more lapsed into silence.

Rose said, "I'm a hard worker, and I learn quickly. Oh, and I'm told I'm a very good cook."

That drew Sanderson's attention. "And you're good with children."

Rose smiled and rolled her eyes. "I'm the eldest of seven children, so I had no choice in that matter." She smiled, but it faded as she felt his eyes on her.

He made her uneasy, although she couldn't say that she felt threatened by him. He was tall and lanky, but despite his gruff manner when they'd first met, he seemed like a quiet and perhaps even gentle man. Sanderson leaned back and folded his arms.

After a while, Rose said, "I'll check on the children."

Sanderson leapt up. "I should be on my way." He stepped outside and called for the children. When they appeared, he sent them to the wagon to wait. "Have you experience keeping house?"

"Only my parents'."

"But you said you could cook."

She smiled. "Aye, I can cook."

"I need someone to look after the children, to clean and cook. Would you be willing?"

"How far away do you live?" she asked.

"Just down the lane within walking distance."

Sanderson nodded. "Good enough."

"And I'll take my pay by the day."

Sanderson's mouth curved at the corner. "All right. Five pence a day then."

Rose looked at him. "Six."

"Would you rob me too, lass?"

"No. But you're wanting a housemaid, a cook, and a nursemaid. I'd say that you're getting a bargain."

"Aye, well, we'll see about that," he said gruffly. "Come by tomorrow before breakfast."

He turned, but Rose said, "Wait!" She disappeared

inside and emerged with a small bundle. "It's the biscuits I promised the children. Please save them until after supper."

He nodded. "Aye. Thank you."

Rose smiled. "Tomorrow."

He smiled for the first time since she had met him. He had quite a nice smile, she decided as he rode away.

IT WASN'T until Sanderson got home that he remembered the purpose of his visit. He had gone to tell that arrogant Alex MacDonell of his intent to take Kenna to court. He didn't need to—the papers would come soon from his solicitor—but he wouldn't be denied the satisfaction of seeing their faces when he told them that their cattle would soon be his.

He thought back on his trip to Fort William. He had seen them herding cattle the day they left home, and it wasn't hard to figure out what they had in mind. So he left the next day for Fort William. After leaving the blacksmith's, he had gone straight to the solicitor, who told him that the courts didn't look kindly upon sales of property that took place within three days of a wedding. In short, he had grounds to take legal action, and he intended to do just that. Alex might have Kenna, but Sanderson would at least have the property that was coming to him.

Sanderson frowned. He wasn't used to being vindictive, and he found it wasn't quite as satisfying as he had expected. But after what they had done to him, it was the least they deserved. He looked back down the road. He could turn around and go to Alex's house, but then he caught sight of his children. The two youngest had fallen asleep, and the three older ones could barely keep their eyes open.

He smiled in spite of himself as he recalled how they had played while he visited with Rose McLeod. He hadn't seen them like that since their mother was alive. He didn't let himself think of her often, for his emotions always welled up then. The next moment, feelings tamped down, he gathered his yawning, sleepy-eyed children and brought them inside. It was a rare moment of calm. He exhaled, poured himself a cup of ale, and indulged in a moment of rest for himself. The papers could wait until tomorrow.

ROSE ARRIVED at dawn with a loaf of fresh bread she had made. the night before, and she got straight to work bringing in a basket of eggs and a pail of milk for breakfast. By the time everyone was back from their early-morning chores, she had breakfast waiting on the table. Sanderson seemed aloof, but he wasn't there to entertain her, so Rose tried to ignore him. The children, in contrast, were not only happy to see her but ate as though they hadn't had a good meal in a long while.

Sanderson wasted no time in finishing his food and going outside to work in the byre. He muttered something about repair work. Rose barely understood him, nor cared to, given his disposition. Instead, she turned to the children with instructions for small household chores for them to do while she got the day's bread started.

By the time Sanderson came in for lunch, the youngest was napping on a box bed in the corner, two others sat playing draughts on a rug by the fire, and the remaining two were building a castle out of wooden blocks. Sanderson stopped in the doorway and took in the sight.

"Is something wrong, Mr. Sanderson?" asked Rose, for he looked truly puzzled.

"No." He shrugged. "Nothing's wrong."

Rose called the children to the table, and they all had fresh bread, cheese, and apples. Sanderson said little to the children and less to Rose as he ate.

"I'll be gone for a time. I must go to the blacksmith in the village." Sanderson cast a sideways glance at Rose then left.

For the first time, she noticed what fine, soft brown eyes he had. Their appeal was well-masked by his brusque manner, but she noticed them just the same. One of the children tugged at her skirt until she turned from the closed door and left behind thoughts of Niall Sanderson.

Kenna rose from the table and reached for Alex's plate, but he seized her waist and pulled her onto his lap.

"Come, lass, give us a kiss." Without waiting, he took it.

Kenna sighed. "I see we'll get nothing accomplished today."

Alex held her close and spoke in low tones. "*Och*, there's a cold wind blowing out there. I'm just doing my best to warm you." His hands strayed from her waist to her breasts.

She took a sharp breath. "You're doing a fine job."

Kenna lifted her chin as Alex kissed his way down her neck. A knock sounded at the door. Kenna started to rise, but Alex tightened his arms about her.

"I've a maid to do that." He kissed her.

"Your maid will catch us if you dinnae release me." Kenna smiled then took in a sharp breath. "Oh, I nearly forgot! I've a letter for you. I brought it back from the village this morning. I'm so sorry I forgot to give it to you sooner."

"I may never forgive you." He took one more kiss before Kenna got up.

Kenna brought him the letter, which he opened and read. She grew concerned as she watched his expression change. "What is it?"

He looked up as the maid entered the room.

"Sir, there's a gentleman asking see you."

Alex went down the hall to the door, where a gentleman waited.

"Mr. Alex MacDonell?"

"Aye," Alex said.

The man handed Alex a letter and left. Alex stared at the envelope with a grim look.

"I heard the door close. Alex? What is it?"

He met Kenna's eyes, which were filled with

concern. "We're to appear at the Fort William Sheriff's Court."

Kenna spoke with an assurance she didn't entirely possess. "Aye. We thought Niall might sue, and he has. But what can he do now? We're married. He cannot undo that."

"No, love, he cannae undo that, but he can undo me."

Kenna glanced down the hall and saw the maid avert her eyes and return to the kitchen. Kenna led Alex to the drawing room, where he sank into a chair. For a long while, he sat without speaking.

"What's the matter? You're scaring me," Kenna said.

He turned to her. "I'm afraid you've made a poor bargain." He had the same look Kenna had seen after he'd had a bad dream—as though all hope was lost.

Kenna said, "I dinnae understand. I thought we could manage a lawsuit."

"So did I."

"Then what's changed?" Kenna touched Alex's hand, but he didn't respond, so she slipped hers away.

"The letter. It was from our friend Duncan."

"What's happened?"

"When he and Jenny sailed for Ireland, he encountered some friends he had sailed with before with the Dutch West India Company. Not long after, they all went to St. Eustatius, where he made his fortune. Before he left, he and I bought a ship. I put nearly all that I had into my share of that ship." He looked blankly at her. "It was wrecked."

Alarmed, Kenna said, "Was he hurt? Has something happened to Jenny?"

"No, he made it to land, but we lost our investment. I've lost everything."

"We're together. We dinnae need money."

"But Sanderson does—and he'll get it from us." Alex stared straight ahead.

Undaunted, Kenna said, "We've got land and livestock. We'll get by for now, and we'll rebuild our fortune."

Alex shook his head. "He could take it all from us —your land and mine. Don't you see? I've ruined us both!" Alex's eyes were rimmed with red as he shook his head and walked out of the house. Kenna called to him as she ran to the door, but he strode to the byre. Soon he rode away, leaving her at the doorway alone.

Minutes later, Kenna heard a gunshot and flinched. It had come from the direction Alex had been riding—from the hill overlooking the loch. There was a place there where the lads used to go to drink whisky. Kenna ran to the byre and saddled her horse. Dread crept through her as she rode. Since he had come home from the war, he had not been himself, but the wedding had been good for him. Or so she'd hoped. But the news about the ship may have been too much to bear.

Kenna rode as fast as she dared over terrain that was rough and steep in places. She arrived at the clearing and called his name. When he failed to answer, she grew frantic. She ran to the place where they used to gather to drink. His horse was tethered there. Fear gripped her, and she felt as though she might be sick to her stomach. Then she saw him hidden by the shadows of trees. On the ground beside him lay his pistol.

She whispered his name, but he didn't turn to her. Kenna drew close behind him and reached out to put her arms about him. He spun about and hooked his arm under her chin.

When he saw it was she, he released her. "God's teeth, Kenna! Dinnae sneak up behind me like that. I might have killed you."

Kenna took a step back.

"Why are you here?" he asked harshly.

"I heard the shot, and I thought—" Kenna stopped herself before she said what she had truly feared. "I thought you were hurt."

His face and voice were void of feeling. "I changed my mind and shot into the air."

"Were you going to hurt yourself?"

He looked at her and did not deny it.

"No! You cannae do that ever!" Kenna pounded her fist on his chest. "No! You promised yourself to me. You cannot hurt yourself!"

He shook his head and stared at the loch.

Kenna took hold of his face. "Look at me, Alex MacDonnell! You will look at me." She couldn't match his strength, but with the sheer force of her will, she commanded his attention. When he met her eyes, she said fiercely, "I love you, and you cannot leave me."

"I've failed you. We've got nothing." He looked at her as if he had already died.

She could barely force out words, for just looking at him broke her heart, but she dug deep and found strength that would have to suffice for the two of them. "You have me. Do you hear me? And I am not nothing." She kissed him hard. "You have me."

With wonder and sadness, he kissed her. "I'm sorry."

He kissed her and kissed her again. He pulled her skirt out of his way as he hoisted her up. Kenna wrapped her legs around him, and he leaned her against the large oak, his strong hands between her and the bark. Kenna clutched at his plaid and his hair as they took one another with savage need. The cold wind whistled through the trees on the side of the hill overlooking the loch.

Chapter 18

To Hope

ROSE SETTLED AN ARGUMENT BETWEEN TWO OF THE children, and after they apologized to each other, she sent them outside to play. She pulled some bread out of the oven next to the fireplace, stood, and turned to find Niall Sanderson staring at her. Rose put a cool hand to her burning cheek before she turned away to resume her duties.

Sanderson went to the door, but he stopped with his hand on the latch. Rose finished wiping the table then went to the fire to lift the black kettle from its hook.

Sanderson approached her and put his hand over hers. "Allow me."

Instead of lifting the kettle, he ran the tips of his fingers over her hand. She stared at his hand as he lifted hers from the kettle handle and let the cloth she held drop to the floor. He lifted her hand to his lips.

Rose looked into his eyes. When he leaned down to kiss her, she put her fingers over his lips to stop him.

"I'll be no man's mistress." She stepped back, her chest heaving as she struggled to calm her heart. "You've food in the kettle and fresh bread from the oven. I'll be leaving now."

As Rose rushed to the door, Sanderson said, "No, wait!"

But she slipped out and ran home. The children called out their good-byes, and Sanderson watched from the door.

IN THE TWO months that followed, Alex and Kenna drew closer, breaking down walls and forging deeper trust. They became stronger together. One evening, Alex lay with his head in her lap while Kenna read by the fire. She set down the book she had been reading to him and combed her slender fingers through his hair. Two days' growth of beard stubbled his face.

"You'll want to shave before going to court in Fort William." She smiled gently.

He glanced at her and grinned. "I'll shave that morning and not a moment before."

"Very well," Kenna said. "But I wish you would think of my face."

He ran his fingers over his cheek. "You're a tender lass, aren't you?"

"Aye, except where you're concerned. If anything threatens you, you'll find I can be quite fierce."

"I'll warn Sanderson then." He sat up and pressed his lips to hers.

Kenna's smiled faded. "Nothing he does can harm us."

Alex kissed her forehead. "I may have to go back to war as a mercenary, but I'll take care of you, no matter what happens."

Kenna said, "You'll not go to war. I won't have it."

Rather than argue, Alex let go of the issue. "There's no point in making plans now."

ROSE TUCKED the last Sanderson child into bed and reached for her arisaid. Mr. Sanderson had been distant and awkward all evening. In fact, all day long he had avoided her. That didn't surprise Rose. It had been weeks since she had spurned his advances. Since then, he had kept a respectable distance, but she still felt awkward around him. He wasn't the sort to force himself upon her, but he was her boss. She had done the right thing, yet she had hoped he would assure her that his feelings were true. He had not, and the truth was she wished that he had.

Sanderson got up from his chair and followed Rose to the door. A bit of her arisaid slipped from her shoulder. Sanderson pulled it back into place, but his hand rested on her shoulder for a moment. He lifted his eyes to meet hers.

"Would you marry me, Mistress McLeod?"

Rose didn't know what to say. His bluntness surprised her, and she had no response. She had tried to deny how her feelings for him had grown since she began working for him, and she loved all of the children. But she had nearly convinced herself not to think of him in that way—until now. "It's so soon."

As if he had not heard her, he said, "Tomorrow I must go to Fort William."

Rose had known nothing of that. Her brows drew together.

He explained, "I must stay overnight. But if you come with me, we could bring the children and marry."

"The children?"

"*Och*, I ken that it's not much of a wedding, but I'll make it up to you later."

Rose didn't know what to say.

"In the meanwhile, we would be together. I have fallen in love with you, Rose."

"Why now? Why are you in such a rush? Why not take time to plan?"

"Does that mean you will?" he asked.

"No, it does not! What it means is I dinnae ken what I mean. This is sudden. I need time—we need time to get to know each other."

Sanderson ran his hands through his hair. "I'm a fool. I was so eager to be with you that I didnae think of how I must seem to you."

"In truth, you confuse me."

He lifted her hand and kissed it. "May I at least hope?"

The soft light in his brown eyes coaxed a smile from her. "Aye, you may hope."

Sanderson grinned. "Thank you."

She laughed. "It is not cause for thanks."

"But it is. For I hadnae thought I would feel this

again." He took her hand, and they sat by the fire. When he had convinced her to call him Niall, he'd told her about his wife and how she died giving birth. "I was certain that love could not happen again for me, so I gave up looking for it. Instead, I sought someone to share my life with—and I found her. Or so I thought."

Rose leaned back and looked about. "Perhaps this isn't the right time…"

"But it is," Niall insisted. "Three days before we were to wed, she ran off with another."

"I'm sorry."

"Alex MacDonell stole her from me."

Rose had heard bits and pieces in the market about Niall's spurned love, but she hadn't realized it was Kenna. She'd stopped listening to gossip when she herself had become the subject of it. Since coming to Glengarry, she'd kept to herself, but her discretion left her stunned by his truth.

"I didnae love her, but I thought I would never know love again, so I accepted that life with her would be different. When she ran off with MacDonnell, she hurt me. What she hurt most of all was my pride."

"Perhaps we should talk about this at another time." Rose got up.

Niall stood and took hold of her shoulders. "Don't you see? It's been different with you. I've felt"—he looked down and swallowed—"love."

All of Rose's good sense disappeared as she looked into his eyes. Their soft warmth brought to life feelings she had hidden.

He said, "Rose, I love you." She started to speak,

but he kissed her. "I'm rushing you. I'm sorry. Just tell me there's hope." His eyes searched hers.

She nodded and smiled. "There is hope."

His eyes brightened. "This calls for a drink to celebrate."

"Celebrate?"

"Hope. It's something I've not felt in a very long time."

Rose smiled as Niall poured two drinks and handed one to her. "To hope then."

THE NEXT MORNING, Rose arrived as she always did, just after dawn. She had slept poorly while her mind raced with thoughts of Niall Sanderson. She had watched him change as his home fell back into order, and she had felt her heart change as she, too, settled into life with his family. It was almost too easy to imagine her life with Niall and his children. But she had been close to marriage before, and she still shied away from the thought of marrying anyone. More than that, there were things he needed to know about her, and knowing them might change his mind. She was drawn to him—that she couldn't deny—but her heart and her mind were at war. She needed time to resolve it. She arrived at his door, and a smile formed on her lips at the thought of seeing him.

Niall answered the door, dressed in his best jacket and plaid.

"Don't you look handsome!" she said as she came

in. His apparent disbelief made her smile. "Aye, you do."

"Well, I must appear presentable."

"Oh? To buy cattle?"

"Buy cattle? What makes you think that?"

Rose blushed. "Oh, I'm sorry. I was tidying up and came across a slip of paper with numbers for heads of cattle. I thought that was why you were going to Fort William."

Niall practically squirmed. "Well, I suppose you should hear it from me."

Given that introduction, Rose was attentive. One of the sleeping children stirred in his bed, so they sat at the table.

Niall quietly told her about his lawsuit. "The law's on my side, for any sale by one of the parties to a treaty of marriage that takes place without the other knowing is evidence of fraud, unless they can rebut it."

"But you've told me you do not love her."

"Aye, but love has nothing to do with it. I was wronged in the eyes of the law."

Rose sat quietly.

"What is it?" asked Niall.

"You've told me you love me."

"I do!"

"If Alex and Kenna had not fallen in love, and if they had not taken the cattle to sell, you and I would never have met," Rose said.

"You're making no sense."

"Twice, I met Alex. First when he was in Fort William to transfer title to Kenna's farm."

"But that had nothing to do with you or me."

"Perhaps not, but I saw him again on his way home after their wedding. He brought me here, and Kenna let me live in her home. I owe them for the life I live now. I owe them for the chance to meet you." Rose leaned back in her chair. "You know nothing about me, yet you think you love me."

"I do love you."

"And what about Kenna?"

"That was a mistake," he said.

"She made a mistake too. Would you condemn her for that?"

"I just want what is fair in the eyes of the law."

"Niall, I have made mistakes too. Before I met you, my parents promised me in marriage. I didnae want to be wed—leastwise to him—so I ran away. I had nowhere to go. I was desperate." She looked into his eyes. "A woman has only so many ways to pay for her food and her shelter."

As her meaning sank in, Niall shook his head slowly.

Rose went on. "I did not do what you're thinking. Alex saved me from that, and he took me home to my family, but the damage was done. People assumed the worst. When my bridegroom rejected me and said I was ruined, my family cast me out. Once more, Alex saved me by bringing me here. And then I met you."

Rose stood. "I imagine that you don't look upon me as you did even moments ago—and I understand. Go to Fort William, and do as you wish. Just know that if your actions hurt that man or his wife, I'll not look upon you in the same way either." Rose went to the fire and stood with her back to him. "Godspeed, Niall."

Chapter 19

The Sheriff's Court

ALEX CRIED OUT IN HIS SLEEP.

Kenna sat up and brushed the damp hair from his forehead, saying softly, "You're with me in Fort William. You've had a bad dream."

He nodded and ran his fingers through his hair. "Aye. I'm all right."

"Yes, you are. And we will be."

He rested his cheek on her forehead and held her. "I'm sorry."

"Shh." Kenna covered his lips with her fingers.

Alex put his hand on hers and pressed his lips into her palm. "You deserve so much more than what I offer you."

"Alex, do you ken how I've loved you? I dinnae think that you do. I've loved you for a long time, and my heart is full. Dinnae tell me you're sorry for that."

His voice broke as he said her name, and he kissed her.

Kenna said, "Now let us get some sleep."

She heard the smile in his voice as he said, "Not just yet."

THEY ARRIVED at the Sheriff's Court the next morning. Niall was there, looking pleased with himself. As they waited, Kenna slipped her hand into Alex's. They shared a fortifying look, but she had known Alex for too long not to see the fear in his eyes. He had always had the quiet reserve that made other men seek him out for advice. He was the stalwart one who would stand to the end, no matter what faced him. But he was troubled, and he saw that as weakness. If she did nothing else in her life, Kenna swore that she would convince him that he was the same man, full of honor and strength, who he always had been. Above all else, no matter what happened in court, he would know that she would always love him and be by his side.

Their case was called. Sanderson stood and looked at Kenna and Alex. His gaze remained fixed upon them until the judge called his name again.

His solicitor opened his mouth, but Sanderson interrupted him. "Your Honor, may I speak?"

The judge gave the solicitor an annoyed look, and he responded with a helpless shrug.

Sanderson said, "Your Honor, I wish to withdraw my complaint."

With her eyes fixed on Sanderson, Kenna grasped Alex's hand.

The judge appeared quite indifferent. "Very well."

Kenna barely heard what the judge said after the case was dismissed. She and Alex shared astonished looks while Sanderson turned to leave the courtroom. On his way out, Sanderson stopped before them, looking strangely pleasant—a look Kenna had rarely seen from him, and certainly not lately.

"You may keep your damned cows." He further stunned Kenna with a warm smile. After that, he walked out of the courtroom with an uncharacteristic spring in his step.

Alex offered Kenna his arm, and they left the courtroom as well. Outside, snow dusted the ground.

Alex turned to Kenna, and his gaze drifted from her lips to her eyes. "If we were not in public, I'd kiss you right now."

"But we are."

"Aye, we are. I've a mind to kiss you anyway," he said with a mischievous grin.

Sanderson mounted his horse and rode past them, his horse kicking up snow and dirt has he raced out of town. Kenna and Alex watched in amazement.

"Has he gone mad?" Kenna asked, laughing.

"He's a man in a hurry."

"He must miss his children." Kenna watched Sanderson disappear over a hill.

Alex shook his head and grinned. "All I care about now is the fresh start he's given the two of us."

"The three of us." Kenna watched as her words sank in.

Alex's brow furrowed with an unspoken question.

Kenna smiled. "Aye."

Alex laughed then pulled Kenna into his arms and swung her about as snow fell about them. When he set her back on the snow-covered ground, the world appeared fresh, giving birth to new hope for their future together.

The Highland Soldiers Series

Highland Soldiers: Scottish historical romances set during turbulence seventeenth century Scotland

Thank You!

Thank you for reading! If you enjoyed this book, please consider leaving a review or a rating. Your feedback on bookstore, Goodreads, and Bookbub websites helps other readers discover books they'll enjoy.

instagram.com/jljarvis.writer

facebook.com/jljarvis1writer

x.com/JLJarvis_writer

youtube.com/@jljarvis-author

goodreads.com/jljarvis

bookbub.com/authors/j-l-jarvis

Also by J.L. Jarvis

Waterfront Summers

(Can be read in any order)

The Cottage at Peregrine Cove

The House on Serenity Lake

Moonlight on Mariner's Bluff

Drake & Wilde Mysteries

(Reading Order)

Love in the Time of Pumpkins

Secrets in the Hollow

Shadow of the Horseman

Standalones

(Can be read in any order)

A Cowboy Kind of Love

A Christmas Eve Stop

Christmas by Lamplight

A Kiss in the Rain

App-ily Ever After

Once Upon a Winter

The Red Rose

Highland Vow

Short Stories

The Holiday Hideaway

Highland Passage

(Can be read in any order)

Highland Passage

Knight Errant

Lost Bride

Highland Soldiers

(Reading Order)

The Enemy

The Betrayal

The Return

The Wanderer

American Hearts

(Can be read in any order)

Secret Hearts

Forbidden Hearts

Runaway Hearts

For more information, visit jljarvis.com.

Get monthly book news at news.jljarvis.com.

About the Author

J.L. Jarvis is a left-handed former opera singer/teacher/lawyer who writes books. She now lives and writes on a mountaintop in upstate New York.

jljarvis.com

www.ingramcontent.com/pod-product-compliance
Lightning Source LLC
Chambersburg PA
CBHW020410210626
46816CB00006BB/2212

* 9 7 8 0 9 9 0 6 4 7 6 3 8 *